Tales from Shakespeare

# Merchant of Venice
# &
# The Comedy of Errors

悅讀莎士比亞故事(6)

威。尼。斯。商。人。

連。環。錯。

Charles and Mary Lamb

# CONTENTS

# CONTENTS

附本

《威尼斯商人》Practice
《連環錯》Practice
《威尼斯商人》中譯
《連環錯》中譯

Principum amicitias

威廉・莎士比亞（William Shakespeare, 1564-1616）

Shakespeare Centre, Henley St, Stratford-upon-Avon, Warwickshire

# 莎士比亞簡介

陳敬旻

威廉·莎士比亞（William Shakespeare）出生於英國的史特拉福（Stratford-upon-Avon）。莎士比亞的父親曾任地方議員，母親是地主的女兒。莎士比亞對婦女在廚房或起居室裡勞動的描繪不少，這大概是經由觀察母親所得。他本人也懂得園藝，故作品中的植草種樹表現鮮活。

1571 年，莎士比亞進入公立學校就讀，校內教學多採拉丁文，因此在其作品中到處可見到羅馬詩人奧維德（Ovid）的影子。當時代古典文學的英譯日漸普遍，有學者認為莎士比亞只懂得英語，但這種說法有可議之處。舉例來說，在高登的譯本裡，森林女神只用 Diana 這個名字，而莎士比亞卻在《仲夏夜之夢》一劇中用奧維德原作中的 Titania 一名來稱呼仙后。和莎士比亞有私交的文學家班·強生（Ben Jonson）則曾說，莎翁「懂得一點拉丁文，和一點點希臘文」。

莎士比亞的劇本亦常引用聖經典故，顯示他對新舊約也頗為熟悉。在伊麗莎白女王時期，通俗英語中已有很多聖經詞語。此外，莎士比亞應該很了解當時年輕人所流行的遊戲娛樂，那時也應該有巡迴劇團不時前來史特拉福演出。 1575 年，伊麗莎白女王來到郡上時，當地人以化裝遊行、假面戲劇、煙火來款待女王，《仲夏夜之夢》裡就有這種盛會的描繪。

1582 年，莎士比亞與安‧海瑟威（Anne Hathaway）結婚，但這場婚姻顯得草率，連莎士比亞的雙親都因不知情而沒有出席婚禮。1586 年，他們在倫敦定居下來。 1586 年的倫敦已是英國首都，年輕人無不想在此大展抱負。史特拉福與倫敦之間的交通頻仍，但對身無長物的人而言，步行仍是最平常的旅行方式。伊麗莎白時期的文學家喜好步行， 1618 年，班‧強生就曾在倫敦與愛丁堡之間徒步來回。

莎士比亞初抵倫敦時的史料不充足，因此引發諸多揣測。其中一說為莎士比亞曾在律師處當職員，因為他在劇本與詩歌中經常提及法律術語。但這種說法站不住腳，因為莎士比亞多有訛用，例如他在《威尼斯商人》和《一報還一報》中提到的法律原理及程序，就有諸多錯誤。

事實上，伊麗莎白時期的作家都喜歡引用法律詞彙，這是因為當時的文人和律師時有往來，而且中產階級也常介入訴訟案件，許多法律術語自然為常人所知。莎士比亞樂於援用法律術語，顯示了他對當代生活和風尚的興趣。莎士比亞自抵達倫敦到告老還鄉，心思始終放在戲劇和詩歌上，不太可能接受法律這門專業領域的訓練。

莎士比亞在倫敦的第一份工作是劇場工作。當時常態營業的劇場有兩個：「劇場」（the Theatre）和「帷幕」（the Curtain）。「劇場」的所有人為詹姆士‧波比奇（James Burbage），莎士比亞就在此落腳。「劇場」財務狀況不佳，1596 年波比奇過世，把「劇場」交給兩個兒子，其中一個兒子便是著名的悲劇演員理查‧波比奇（Richard Burbage）。後來「劇場」因租約問題無法解決，決定將原有的建築物拆除，在泰晤士河對面重建，改名為「環球」（the Globe）。不久，「環球」就展開了戲劇史上空前繁榮的時代。

伊麗莎白時期的戲劇表演只有男演員，所有的女性角色都由男性擔任。演員反串時會戴上面具，效果十足，然而這並不損故事的意境。莎士比亞本身也是一位出色的演員，曾在《皆大歡喜》和《哈姆雷特》中分別扮演忠僕亞當和國王鬼魂這兩個角色。

莎士比亞很留意演員的説白道詞，這點可從哈姆雷特告誡伶人的對話中窺知一二。莎士比亞熟稔劇場的技術與運作，加上他也是劇場股東，故對劇場的營運和組織都甚有研究。不過，他的志業不在演出或劇場管理，而是劇本和詩歌創作。

莎士比亞的戲劇創作始於 1591 年，他當時真正師法的對象是擅長喜劇的約翰・李利（John Lyly），以及曾寫下轟動一時的悲劇《帖木兒大帝》（*Tamburlaine the Great*）的克里斯多夫・馬婁（Christopher Marlowe）。莎翁戲劇的特色是兼容並蓄，吸收各家長處，而且他也勤奮多產。一直到 1611 年封筆之前，他每年平均寫出兩部劇作和三卷詩作。莎士比亞慣於在既有的文學作品中尋找材料，又重視大眾喜好，常能讓平淡無奇的作品廣受喜愛。

在當時，劇本都是賣斷給劇場，不能再賣給出版商，因此莎劇的出版先後，並不能反映其創作的時間先後。莎翁作品的先後順序都由後人所推斷，推測的主要依據是作品題材和韻格。他早期的戲劇作品，無論悲劇或喜劇，性質都很單純。隨著創作的手法逐漸成熟，內容愈來愈複雜深刻，悲喜劇熔冶一爐。

自 1591 年席德尼爵士（Sir Philip Sidney）的十四行詩集發表後，十四行詩（sonnets，另譯為商籟）在英國即普遍受到文人的喜愛與仿傚。其中許多作品承續佩脫拉克（Petrarch）的風格，多描寫愛情的酸甜苦樂。莎士比亞的創作一向很能反應當時代的文學風尚，在詩歌體裁鼎盛之時，他也將才華展現在十四行詩上，並將部分作品寫入劇本之中。

莎士比亞的十四行詩主要有兩個主題：婚姻責任和詩歌的不朽。這兩者皆是文藝復興時期詩歌中常見的主題。不少人以為莎士比亞的十四行詩表達了他個人的自省與懺悔，但事實上這些內容有更多是源於他的戲劇天分。

1595 年至 1598 年，莎士比亞陸續寫了《羅密歐與茱麗葉》、《仲夏夜之夢》、《馴悍記》、《威尼斯商人》和若干歷史劇，他的詩歌戲劇也在這段時期受到肯定。當時代的梅爾斯（Francis Meres）就將莎士比亞視為最偉大的文學家，他說：「要是繆思會說英語，一定也會喜歡引用莎士比亞的精彩語藻。」「無論悲劇或喜劇，莎士比亞的表現都是首屈一指。」

闊別故鄉十一年後，莎士比亞於 1596 年返回故居，並在隔年買下名為「新居」（New Place）的房子。那是鎮上第二大的房子，他大幅改建整修，爾後家道日益興盛。莎士比亞有足夠的財力置產並不足以為奇，但他大筆的固定收入主要來自表演，而非劇本創作。當時不乏有成功的演員靠演戲發財，甚至有人將這種現象寫成劇本。

除了表演之外，劇場行政及管理的工作，還有宮廷演出的賞賜，都是他的財源。許多文獻均顯示，莎士比亞是個非常關心財富、地產和社會地位的人，讓許多人感到與他的詩人形象有些扞格不入。

伊麗莎白女王過世後，詹姆士一世（James I）於 1603 年登基，他把莎士比亞所屬的劇團納入保護。莎士比亞此時寫了《第十二夜》和佳評如潮的《哈姆雷特》，成就傲視全英格蘭。但他仍謙恭有禮、溫文爾雅，一如十多前年初抵倫敦的樣子，因此也愈發受到大眾的喜愛。

從這一年起，莎士比亞開始撰寫悲劇《奧賽羅》。他寫悲劇並非是因為精神壓力或生活變故，而是身為一名劇作家，最終目的就是要寫出優秀的悲劇作品。當時他嘗試以詩入劇，在《哈姆雷特》和《一報還一報》中尤其爐火純青。隨後《李爾王》和《馬克白》問世，一直到四年後的《安東尼與克麗奧佩脫拉》，寫作風格登峰造極。

1609 年，倫敦瘟疫猖獗，隔年不見好轉，46 歲的莎士比亞決定告別倫敦，返回史特拉福退隱。 1616 年，莎士比亞和老友德雷頓、班・強生聚會時，可能由於喝得過於盡興，回家後發高燒，一病不起。他將遺囑修改完畢，同年 4 月 23 日，恰巧在他 52 歲的生日當天去世。

七年後，昔日的劇團好友收錄他的劇本做為全集出版，其中有喜劇、歷史劇、悲劇等共 36 個劇本。此書不僅不負莎翁本人所託，也為後人留下珍貴而豐富的文化資源，其中不僅包括美妙動人的詞句，還有各種人物的性格塑造，如高貴、低微、嚴肅或歡樂等性格的著墨。

除了作品，莎士比亞本人也在生前受到讚揚。班‧強生曾說他是個「正人君子，天性開放自由，想像力出奇，擁有大無畏的思想，言詞溫和，蘊含機智。」也有學者以勇敢、敏感、平衡、幽默和身心健康這五種特質來形容莎士比亞，並說他「將無私的愛奉為至上，認為罪惡的根源是恐懼，而非金錢。」

值得一提的是，有人認為這些劇本刻畫入微，具有知性，不可能是未受過大學教育的莎士比亞所寫，因而引發爭議。有人就此推測真正的作者，其中較為人知的有法蘭西斯‧培根（Francis Bacon）和牛津的德維爾公爵（Edward de Vere of Oxford），後者形成了頗具影響力的牛津學派。儘管傳說繪聲繪影，各種假說和研究不斷，但大概已經沒有人會懷疑確有莎士比亞這個人的存在了。

# 作者簡介：蘭姆姐弟

陳敬旻

姐姐瑪麗（Mary Lamb）生於 1764 年，弟弟查爾斯（Charles Lamb）於 1775 年也在倫敦呱呱落地。因為家境不夠寬裕，瑪麗沒有接受過完整的教育。她從小就做針線活，幫忙持家，照顧母親。查爾斯在學生時代結識了詩人柯立芝（Samuel Taylor Coleridge），兩人成為終生的朋友。查爾斯後來因家中經濟困難而輟學， 1792 年轉而就職於東印度公司（East India House），這是他謀生的終身職業。

查爾斯在二十歲時一度精神崩潰，瑪麗則因為長年工作過量，在 1796 年突然精神病發，持刀攻擊父母，母親不幸傷重身亡。這件人倫悲劇發生後，瑪麗被判為精神異常，送往精神病院。查爾斯為此放棄自己原本期待的婚姻，以便全心照顧姐姐，使她免於在精神病院終老。

十九世紀的英國教育重視莎翁作品，一般的中產階級家庭也希望孩子早點接觸莎劇。1806 年，文學家兼編輯高德溫（William Godwin）邀請查爾斯協助「少年圖書館」的出版計畫，請他將莎翁的劇本改寫為適合兒童閱讀的故事。

查爾斯接受這項工作後就與瑪麗合作，他負責六齣悲劇，瑪麗負責十四齣喜劇並撰寫前言。瑪麗在後來曾描述說，他們兩人「就坐在同一張桌子上改寫，看起來就好像《仲夏夜之夢》裡的荷米雅與海蓮娜一樣。」就這樣，姐弟兩人合力完成了這一系列的莎士比亞故事。《莎士比亞故事集》在 1807 年出版後便大受好評，建立了查爾斯的文學聲譽。

查爾斯的寫作風格獨特，筆
法樸實，主題豐富。他將自
己的一生，包括童年時代、
基督教會學校的生活、東印
度公司的光陰、與瑪麗相伴
的點點滴滴，以及自己的白
日夢、鍾愛的書籍和友人等
等，都融入在文章裡，作品
充滿細膩情感和豐富的想像
力。他的軟弱、怪異、魅
力、幽默、口吃，在在都使
讀者感到親切熟悉，而獨特
的筆法與敘事方式，也使他
成為英國出色的散文大師。

1823 年，查爾斯和瑪麗領養了一個孤兒愛瑪。兩年後，查爾斯自東
印度公司退休，獲得豐厚的退休金。查爾斯的健康情形和瑪麗的精
神狀況卻每況愈下。 1833 年，愛瑪嫁給出版商後，又只剩下姐弟兩
人。 1834 年 7 月，由於幼年時代的好友柯立芝去世，查爾斯的精神
一蹶不振，沉湎酒精。此年秋天，查爾斯在散步時不慎跌倒，傷及
顏面，後來傷口竟惡化至不可收拾的地步，而於年底過世。

查爾斯善與人交，他和同時期的許多文人都保持良好情誼，又因他
一生對姐姐的照顧不餘遺力，所以也廣受敬佩。查爾斯和瑪麗兩人
都終生未婚，查爾斯曾在一篇伊利亞小品中，將他們的狀況形容為
「雙重單身」（double singleness）。查爾斯去世後，瑪麗的心理狀態
雖然漸趨惡化，但仍繼續活了十三年之久。

# Merchant of Venice

威尼斯商人

# 導讀

## 故事的來源

《威尼斯商人》又名《威尼斯的猶太人》（*The Jew of Venice*）。這齣戲於 1598 年首演，可能是莎士比亞在 1596-97 年間寫成的，主要情節由兩個常見的故事改編而成：

1 巴薩紐和波兒榭的故事：從一本名為 Il Pecorone（意指「大綿羊」或「笨蛋」）的義大利故事集之中獲得靈感。

2 賽拉客向安東尼索求一磅肉作為賠償的故事：有多個來源，其中之一是 1596 年出版的《雄辯家》（*The Orator*）英譯本，作者為希爾維（Alexander Silvayn）。

猶太人取基督徒的肉並在逾越節（Passover）食用的說法，在中古時代早期就已流傳。基督徒相信猶太人曾加害耶穌基督，在伊莉莎白時期的劇場舞台上，賽拉客總是留著紅鬍鬚，長著鷹鉤鼻，模樣十足邪惡。莎翁當時代的人普遍認為：除非猶太人放棄其異教信仰和行為，否則基督徒很難原諒或接納他們。

THE MERCHANT of VENICE

文藝復興時期的歐洲人一提起猶太人，就聯想到放高利貸。在當時，放高利貸已經是一普遍的生財之道，只是一般人在情緒上仍對其反感。他們認為放高利貸是道德上的罪行，這種獲利手段和經商不一樣，不需才智本錢，就可以賺取暴利，有時甚至近乎違法，而放高利貸的人的普遍形象則是腐敗、貪婪、吝嗇。

早於莎翁三百年的英王愛德華一世（Edward I, 在位其間為 1272-1307 年）就曾下令將猶太人逐出英國，但在伊莉莎白時期，仍有部分猶太人居住在倫敦，只是他們礙於民風政令，必須隱瞞自己的身分及宗教信仰。

1589 年，英國劇作家馬婁（Christopher Marlowe）所寫的《馬爾他的猶太人》（*The Jew of Malta*）演出後，可能對莎士比亞造成了影響。馬婁所描寫的猶太人白若巴（Barabas）是個不折不扣的惡棍，為求目的不擇手段。白若巴在劇中沒有敵手，只有戲外的觀眾能譴責他。莎士比亞所描寫的賽拉客則有所不同。

## 猶太人角色

莎翁的賽拉客這一角色塑造得完整而真實。他頭腦精明，行事謹慎，口才流利，以放高利貸大發橫財，讓基督徒有憎恨他的理由。其中的衝突不只有種族和財務問題，也象徵了兩種全然不同的宗教、生活和價值觀。賽拉客過著節制吝嗇的生活，輕蔑基督徒生活的奢華浪費。事實上，在當時就常見威尼斯商人穿著華麗，宛如王室貴族。

另外，對賽拉客而言，善人的定義是經濟狀況足以維生，其他的道德或抽象的價值觀則毫無意義。劇中的基督徒與賽拉客代表完全不同的兩種人物，例如，巴薩紐因生活奢侈，阮囊羞澀，為攀闊親事，只得向好友借錢，好友則為其赴湯蹈火在所不惜，而賽拉客卻對金錢以外的東西都無動於衷。

## 波兒榭的角色

波兒榭所居住的背芒特（Belmont）在本劇中象徵一個不尋常的地點，這個地名的意思是「美麗的山丘」。當地平靜和諧，和擁擠紛亂、斤斤計較的威尼斯形成強烈對比。

波兒榭的住所象徵井然有序、物質生活不乏，而波兒榭本人更是具有理想的基督徒形象。她慷慨奉獻，洞察力敏銳，具有活力，反應靈敏。賽拉客僅依借據所載，不容變更。她以其人之道還治其人之身，致使賽拉客依約不得讓安東尼留下半滴血。這種破解的手法在當時很盛傳，也因此，莎翁主要要呈現的並不是令人激賞的機智，而是要表現波兒榭戰勝了邪惡。

除此之外，《威尼斯商人》也對愛情和友情多所著墨。曾有人試圖以同性戀來詮釋安東尼與巴薩紐之間的情誼，因為兩人都曾表示對方的性命勝於自己。儘管有這種指涉，但眾人最後返回背芒特的那一幕，似乎又暗示愛情更勝友情一籌。

波兒榭是本劇的女性靈魂人物，和賽拉客特別互相托襯。在故事中，基督徒對於批評持開放態度，猶太人則嚴守自己的行為準則。伊莉莎白時期，波兒榭較常成為此劇的核心人物。到了十九世紀，賽拉客卻時常躍昇為主角，使其他角色黯然失色，甚至連最後在背芒特的逗趣一幕都被刪掉。評論家史鐸爾（E. E. Stoll）表示，伊莉莎白時期的民眾對吝嗇、放高利貸的猶太人存有根深柢固的偏見，故不足以成為本劇的中心人物。不過，賽拉客仍大受劇場演員的歡迎。

## 舞台上的搬演

舞台上詮釋賽拉客的方式有多種。他時而代表魔鬼的化身，時而成為喜劇裡的惡棍，偶爾也會展現受到曲解與委屈的可憐形象，引起觀眾的同情，蒙上了一層悲劇色彩。這種訴諸情感的詮釋手法由1814 年英國演員愛德蒙 金（Edmund Kean）首創，其後也影響了勞倫斯 ‧ 奧利佛對這個角色的詮釋。

現代的劇場則傾向於將賽拉客塑造成一名受害人。他因周遭人對宗教抱持偏執頑固的立場而被誤解。這尤其表現在他自辯的那一段話上：難道因為宗教信仰不同，他就應該受到他人的道德倫理準則所批判嗎？莎士比亞以這段話呈現出賽拉客的人性。

二十世紀以後，《威尼斯商人》因對猶太人的偏見而引發不少種族議題，特別是二次世界大戰之後，此劇已轉為問題劇，多數人不再以輕鬆的眼光看待這個故事，原來的喜劇成分也就消失無蹤了。

## 人物表

| Shylock | 賽拉客 | 一位放高利貸的猶太人 |
| Antonio | 安東尼 | 一位年輕的威尼斯商人 |
| Bassanio | 巴薩紐 | 安東尼的好友 |
| Portia | 波兒榭 | 巴薩紐的未婚妻 |
| Gratiano | 葛提諾 | 巴薩紐的友人 |
| Nerissa | 涅芮莎 | 波兒榭的貼身侍女 |

Shylock, the Jew, lived at Venice. He was an usurer[1], who had amassed[2] an immense fortune by lending money at great interest to Christian merchants.

Shylock, being a hard-hearted man, exacted the payment of the money he lent with such severity[3] that he was much disliked by all good men, and particularly by Antonio, a young merchant of Venice; and Shylock as much hated Antonio, because he used to lend money to people in distress, and would never take any interest for the money he lent; therefore there was great enmity[4] between this covetous[5] Jew and the generous merchant Antonio. Whenever Antonio met Shylock on the Rialto[6](or Exchange), he used to reproach[7] him with his usuries and hard dealings, which the Jew would bear with seeming patience, while he secretly meditated revenge.

1 usurer [ˈjuːʒərər] (n.) 放高利貸者
2 amass [əˈmæs] (v.) 積聚財富
3 severity [sɪˈverɪti] (n.) 嚴厲
4 enmity [ˈenmɪti] (n.) 仇恨
5 covetous [ˈkʌvɪtəs] (a.) 貪圖的
6 Rialto [rɪˈælto] (n.) 交易場所
7 reproach [rɪˈproʊtʃ] (v.) 斥責

*Shylock*

Antonio was the kindest man that lived, the best conditioned, and had the most unwearied spirit in doing courtesies; indeed, he was one in whom the ancient Roman honor more appeared than in any that drew breath in Italy. He was greatly beloved by all his fellow-citizens; but the friend who was nearest and dearest to his heart was Bassanio, a noble Venetian, who, having but a small patrimony[8], had nearly exhausted his little fortune by living in too expensive a manner for his slender means, as young men of high rank with small fortunes are too apt to do. Whenever Bassanio wanted money, Antonio assisted him; and it seemed as if they had but one heart and one purse between them.

One day Bassanio came to Antonio, and told him that he wished to repair his fortune by a wealthy marriage with a lady whom he dearly loved, whose father, that was lately dead, had left her sole heiress to a large estate; and that in her father's lifetime he used to visit at her house, when he thought he had observed this lady had sometimes from her eyes sent speechless messages, that seemed to say he would be no unwelcome suitor; but not having money to furnish himself with an appearance befitting the lover of so rich an heiress, he besought Antonio to add to the many favors he had shown him, by lending him three thousand ducats[9].

8 patrimony ['pætrɪmoʊni] (n.) 祖產
9 ducat ['dʌkət] (n.) 舊時流通於歐洲、價值不一的金銀幣

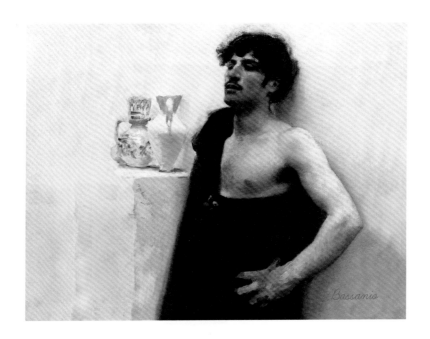

Bassanio

 Antonio had no money by him at that time to
lend his friend; but expecting soon to have some
ships come home laden with merchandise, he said
he would go to Shylock, the rich moneylender, and
borrow the money upon the credit of those ships.

Antonio and Bassanio went together to Shylock,
and Antonio asked the Jew to lend him three
thousand ducats upon any interest he should require,
to be paid out of the merchandise contained in his
ships at sea.

Antonio_reproaching_Shylock

On this, Shylock thought within himself: "If I can once catch him on the hip, I will feed fat the ancient grudge[10] I bear him, he hates our Jewish nation; he lends out money gratis[11]; and among the merchants he rails[12] at me and my well-earned bargains, which he calls interest. Cursed be my tribe if I forgive him!"

Antonio finding he was musing[13] within himself and did not answer, and being impatient for the money, said: "Shylock, do you hear? Will you lend the money?"

10 grudge [grʌdʒ] (n.) 怨恨
11 gratis ['gretɪs] (adv.) 免費地
12 rail [reɪl] (v.) 抱怨；責罵
13 muse ['mjuːz] (v.) 沈思

🎧5 To this question the Jew replied: "Signior Antonio, on the Rialto many a time and often you have railed at me about my moneys and my usuries, and I have borne it with a patient shrug, for sufferance is the badge[14] of all our tribe; and then you have called me unbeliever, cut-throat dog, and spit upon my Jewish garments, and spurned[15] at me with your foot, as if I was a cur[16]. Well, then, it now appears you need my help, and you come to me, and say, 'Shylock, lend me moneys.' Has a dog money? Is it possible a cur should lend three thousand ducats? Shall I bend low and say, 'Fair sir, you spit upon me on Wednesday last, another time you called me dog, and for these courtesies I am to lend you moneys.'"

Antonio replied: "I am as like to call you so again, to spit on you again, and spurn you, too. If you will lend me this money, lend it not to me as to a friend, but rather lend it to me as to an enemy, that, if I break, you may with better face exact the penalty."

"Why, look you," said Shylock, "how you storm! I would be friends with you and have your love. I will forget the shames you have put upon me. I will supply your wants and take no interest for my money."

14 badge [bædʒ] (n.) 象徵；代表
15 spurn [spɜːrn] (v.) 輕蔑地拒絕；擯斥
16 cur [kɜːr] (n.) 行為卑劣者

🎧 6  This seemingly kind offer greatly surprised Antonio; and then Shylock, still pretending kindness and that all he did was to gain Antonio's love, again said he would lend him the three thousand ducats, and take no interest for his money; only Antonio should go with him to a lawyer and there sign in merry sport a bond[17], that if he did not repay the money by a certain day, he would forfeit[18] a pound of flesh, to be cut off from any part of his body that Shylock pleased.

"Content," said Antonio, "I will sign to this bond, and say there is much kindness in the Jew."

17 bond [bɑːnd] (n.) 字據
18 forfeit ['fɔːrfit] (v.) 喪失

🎧 Bassanio said Antonio should not sign to such a bond for him; but still Antonio insisted that he would sign it, for that before the day of payment came, his ships would return laden with many times the value of the money.

Shylock, hearing this debate, exclaimed: "O, father Abraham, what suspicious people these Christians are! Their own hard dealings teach them to suspect the thoughts of others. I pray you tell me this, Bassanio: if he should break his day, what should I gain by the exaction of the forfeiture? A pound of man's flesh, taken from a man, is not so estimable[19], nor profitable, neither, as the flesh of mutton or beef. I say, to buy his favor I offer this friendship: if he will take it, so; if not, adieu."

At last, against the advice of Bassanio, who, notwithstanding all the Jew had said of his kind intentions, did not like his friend should run the hazard[20] of this shocking penalty for his sake, Antonio signed the bond, thinking it really was (as the Jew said) merely in sport.

19 estimable ['estɪməbəl] (a.) 有價值的
20 hazard ['hæzərd] (n.) 危險

🎧⁸ The rich heiress that Bassanio wished to marry lived near Venice, at a place called Belmont. Her name was Portia, and in the graces of her person and her mind she was nothing inferior to that Portia, of whom we read, who was Cato's daughter and the wife of Brutus.

Bassanio being so kindly supplied with money by his friend Antonio, at the hazard of his life, set out for Belmont with a splendid train and attended by a gentleman of the name of Gratiano.

Bassanio proving successful in his suit, Portia in a short time consented to accept of him for a husband.

Bassanio confessed to Portia that he had no fortune and that his high birth and noble ancestry was all that he could boast of; she, who loved him for his worthy qualities and had riches enough not to regard wealth in a husband, answered, with a graceful modesty, that she would wish herself a thousand times more fair, and ten thousand times more rich, to be more worthy of him; and then the accomplished Portia prettily dispraised herself, and said she was an unlessoned girl, unschooled, unpracticed, yet not so old but that she could learn, and that she would commit her gentle spirit to be directed and governed by him in all things; and she said:

PORTIA.   By my troth, Nerissa, my little body is aweary of
this great world.

"Myself and what is mine to you and yours is now converted[21]. But yesterday, Bassanio, I was the lady of this fair mansion, queen of myself, and mistress over these servants; and now this house, these servants, and myself, are yours, my lord; I give them with this ring," presenting a ring to Bassanio.

Bassanio was so overpowered with gratitude and wonder at the gracious manner in which the rich and noble Portia accepted of a man of his humble fortunes that he could not express his joy and reverence[22] to the dear lady who so honored him, by anything but broken words of love and thankfulness; and, taking the ring, he vowed never to part with it.

Gratiano and Nerissa, Portia's waiting-maid, were in attendance upon their lord and lady, when Portia so gracefully promised to become the obedient wife of Bassanio; and Gratiano, wishing Bassanio and the generous lady joy, desired permission to be married at the same time.

"With all my heart, Gratiano," said Bassanio, "if you can get a wife."

21 convert [kən'vɜːrt] (v.) 使轉變
22 reverence ['revərəns] (n.) 尊敬；敬畏之情

🎧10  Gratiano then said that he loved the Lady Portia's fair waiting-gentlewoman, Nerissa, and that she had promised to be his wife if her lady married Bassanio. Portia asked Nerissa if this was true.

Nerissa replied: "Madam, it is so, if you approve of it."

Portia willingly consenting[23], Bassanio pleasantly said: "Then our wedding-feast shall be much honored by your marriage, Gratiano."

---

23 consent [kən'sent] (v.) 同意

🎧 11  The happiness of these lovers was sadly crossed[24] at this moment by the entrance of a messenger, who brought a letter from Antonio containing fearful tidings[25].

When Bassanio read Antonio's letter, Portia feared it was to tell him of the death of some dear friend, he looked so pale; and, enquiring what was the news which had so distressed him, he said: "Oh, sweet Portia, here are a few of the unpleasantest words that ever blotted[26] paper! Gentle lady, when I first imparted[27] my love to you, I freely told you all the wealth I had ran in my veins; but I should have told you that I had less than nothing, being in debt."

Bassanio then told Portia what has been here related[28], of his borrowing the money of Antonio, and of Antonio's procuring[29] it of Shylock the Jew, and of the bond by which Antonio had engaged to forfeit a pound of flesh, if it was not repaid by a certain day: and then Bassanio read Antonio's letter, the words of which were:

24 cross [krɔːs] (v.) 反對；阻礙
25 tidings ['taɪdɪŋz] (n.) 消息；音信
26 blot [blɑːt] (v.) 在（紙上）弄點墨水
27 impart [ɪm'pɑːrt] (v.) 通知；告知
28 relate [rɪ'leɪt] (v.) 講述
29 procure [pro'kjʊr] (v.) 獲得；取得

🎧12 *'Sweet Bassanio, my ships are all lost, my bond to the Jew is forfeited, and since in paying it is impossible I should live, I could wish to see you at my death; notwithstanding, use your pleasure. If your love for me do not persuade you to come, let not my letter.'*

"Oh, my dear love," said Portia, "despatch[30] all business and begone; you shall have gold to pay the money twenty times over, before this kind friend shall lose a hair by my Bassanio's fault; and as you are so dearly bought, I will dearly love you."

Portia then said she would be married to Bassanio before he set out, to give him a legal right to her money; and that same day they were married, and Gratiano was also married to Nerissa; and Bassanio and Gratiano, the instant they were married, set out in great haste for Venice, where Bassanio found Antonio in prison.

30 despatch [dɪˈspætʃ] (v.) 迅速結束；打發

ANTONIO.  I pray thee, hear me speak.
SHYLOCK.  I'll have my bond; I will not hear thee speak.

Act. 3  Scene. 3

The day of payment being past, the cruel Jew would not accept of the money which Bassanio offered him, but insisted upon having a pound of Antonio's flesh. A day was appointed to try this shocking cause before the Duke of Venice, and Bassanio awaited in dreadful suspense the event of the trial.

（14）   When Portia parted with her husband, she spoke cheeringly to him and bade him bring his dear friend along with him when he returned; yet she feared it would go hard with Antonio, and when she was left alone, she began to think and consider within herself if she could by any means be instrumental[31] in saving the life of her dear Bassanio's friend. And notwithstanding when she wished to honor her Bassanio, she had said to him, with such a meek[32] and wifelike grace, that she would submit in all things to be governed by his superior wisdom, yet being now called forth into action by the peril[33] of her honored husband's friend, she did nothing doubt her own powers, and by the sole guidance of her own true and perfect judgement at once resolved to go herself to Venice and speak in Antonio's defence.

Portia had a relation who was a counselor in the law; to this gentleman, whose name was Bellario, she wrote, and, stating the case to him, desired his opinion, and that with his advice he would also send her the dress worn by a counselor.

---

31 instrumental [ˌɪnstrəˈmentəl] (a.) 有幫助的
32 meek [miːk] (a.) 溫順的
33 peril [ˈperəl] (n.) 危險

🎧15　When the messenger returned, he brought letters from Bellario of advice how to proceed, and also everything necessary for her equipment.

　　Portia dressed herself and her maid Nerissa in men's apparel[34], and putting on the robes of a counselor, she took Nerissa along with her as her clerk; and setting out immediately, they arrived at Venice on the very day of the trial.

34 apparel [ə'pærəl] (n.) 服裝

🎧16　The cause was just going to be heard before the Duke and senators of Venice in the senate-house, when Portia entered this high court of justice and presented a letter from Bellario, in which that learned counselor wrote to the duke, saying he would have come himself to plead[35] for Antonio but that he was prevented by sickness, and he requested that the learned young doctor Balthasar (so he called Portia) might be permitted to plead in his stead[36].

This the Duke granted, much wondering at the youthful appearance of the stranger, who was prettily disguised by her counselor's robes and her large wig.

And now began this important trial. Portia looked around her and she saw the merciless Jew; and she saw Bassanio, but he knew her not in her disguise. He was standing beside Antonio, in an agony[37] of distress and fear for his friend.

---

35 plead [pliːd] (v.) 為某人辯護
36 stead [sted] (n.) 代替
37 agony ['ægəni] (n.) 極大的痛苦

🎧 The importance of the arduous[38] task Portia had engaged in gave this tender lady courage, and she boldly proceeded in the duty she had undertaken to perform. And first of all she addressed herself to Shylock; and allowing that he had a right by the Venetian law to have the forfeit expressed in the bond, she spoke so sweetly of the noble quality of MERCY as would have softened any heart but the unfeeling Shylock's, saying that it dropped as the gentle rain from heaven upon the place beneath; and how mercy was a double blessing, it blessed him that gave and him that received it; and how it became monarchs[39] better than their crowns, being an attribute[40] of God himself; and that earthly power came nearest to God's in proportion as mercy tempered[41] justice; and she bade Shylock remember that as we all pray for mercy, that same prayer should teach us to show mercy.

Shylock only answered her by desiring to have the penalty forfeited in the bond.

"Is he not able to pay the money?" asked Portia.

38 arduous ['ɑːrdʒuəs] (a.) 艱鉅的；困難的
39 monarch ['mɑːnərk] (n.) 君主
40 attribute [əˈtrɪbjuːt] (n.) 性質；屬性
41 temper ['tempər] (v.) 緩和；使軟化

🎧18 Bassanio then offered the Jew the payment of the three thousand ducats as many times over as he should desire; which Shylock refusing, and still insisting upon having a pound of Antonio's flesh, Bassanio begged the learned young counselor would endeavor to wrest[42] the law a little, to save Antonio's life. But Portia gravely answered that laws once established must never be altered.

Shylock, hearing Portia say that the law might not be altered, it seemed to him that she was pleading in his favor, and he said: "A Daniel is come to judgment! O wise young judge, how I do honor you! How much elder are you than your looks!"

Portia now desired Shylock to let her look at the bond; and when she had read it she said: "This bond is forfeited, and by this the Jew may lawfully claim a pound of flesh, to be by him cut off nearest Antonio's heart." Then she said to Shylock, "Be merciful; take the money and bid me tear the bond."

But no mercy would the cruel Shylock show; and he said, "By my soul, I swear there is no power in the tongue of man to alter me."

42 wrest [rest] (v.) 歪曲；曲解

🎧19 "Why, then, Antonio," said Portia, "you must prepare your bosom for the knife." And while Shylock was sharpening a long knife with great eagerness to cut off the pound of flesh, Portia said to Antonio, "Have you anything to say?"

Antonio with a calm resignation[43] replied that he had but little to say, for that he had prepared his mind for death. Then he said to Bassanio: "Give me your hand, Bassanio! Fare you well! Grieve not that I am fallen into this misfortune for you. Commend me to your honorable wife and tell her how I have loved you!"

---

43 resignation [ˌrezɪɡˈneɪʃən] (n.) 聽任；順從

🎧 20 Bassanio in the deepest affliction[44] replied: "Antonio, I am married to a wife who is as dear to me as life itself; but life itself, my wife, and all the world are not esteemed with me above your life. I would lose all, I would sacrifice all to this devil here, to deliver[45] you."

Portia hearing this, though the kind-hearted lady was not at all offended with her husband for expressing the love he owed to so true a friend as Antonio in these strong terms, yet could not help answering: "Your wife would give you little thanks, if she were present, to hear you make this offer."

And then Gratiano, who loved to copy what his lord did, thought he must make a speech like Bassanio's, and he said, in Nerissa's hearing, who was writing in her clerk's dress by the side of Portia: "I have a wife whom I protest I love. I wish she were in heaven if she could but entreat[46] some power there to change the cruel temper of this currish Jew."

"It is well you wish this behind her back, else you would have but an unquiet house," said Nerissa.

Shylock now cried out impatiently: "We trifle time. I pray pronounce the sentence."

---

44 affliction [əˈflɪkʃən] (n.) 痛苦
45 deliver [dɪˈlɪvər] (v.) 解救;釋放
46 entreat [ɪnˈtriːt] (v.) 懇求

And now all was awful expectation in the court, and every heart was full of grief for Antonio.

Portia asked if the scales were ready to weigh the flesh; and she said to the Jew, "Shylock, you must have some surgeon by, lest he bleed to death."

Shylock, whose whole intent was that Antonio should bleed to death, said, "It is not so named in the bond."

Portia replied: "It is not so named in the bond, but what of that? It were good you did so much for charity."

To this all the answer Shylock would make was, "I cannot find it; it is not in the bond."

"Then," said Portia, "a pound of Antonio's flesh is thine. The law allows it and the court awards it. And you may cut this flesh from off his breast. The law allows it and the court awards it."

Again Shylock exclaimed: "O wise and upright[47] judge! A Daniel is come to judgment!" And then he sharpened his long knife again, and looking eagerly on Antonio, he said, "Come, prepare!"

47 upright ['ʌpraɪt] (a.) 正直的

PORTIA.    Have by some surgeon, Shylock, on your charge,
                 To stop his wounds, lest he do bleed to death.
SHYLOCK.   Is it so nominated in the bond?

(22) "Tarry[48] a little, Jew," said Portia. "There is something else. This bond here gives you no drop of blood; the words expressly are, 'a pound of flesh'. If in the cutting off the pound of flesh you shed one drop of Christian blood, your lands and goods are by the law to be confiscated[49] to the state of Venice."

Now as it was utterly impossible for Shylock to cut off the pound of flesh without shedding some of Antonio's blood, this wise discovery of Portia's, that it was flesh and not blood that was named in the bond, saved the life of Antonio; and all admiring the wonderful sagacity[50] of the young counselor who had so happily thought of this expedient[51], plaudits[52] resounded from every part of the senate-house; and Gratiano exclaimed, in the words which Shylock had used: "O wise and upright judge! Mark, Jew, a Daniel is come to judgment!"

48 tarry ['tæri] (v.) 停留；逗留
49 confiscate ['kɔːnfɪskeɪt] (v.) 充公；沒收
50 sagacity [sə'gæsɪti] (n.) 精明；睿智
51 expedient [ɪk'spiːdiənt] (n.) 權宜之計
52 plaudit ['plɔːdɪts] (n.) 喝采；鼓掌

🎧23 Shylock, finding himself defeated in his cruel intent, said, with a disappointed look, that he would take the money. And Bassanio, rejoiced beyond measure at Antonio's unexpected deliverance, cried out: "Here is the money!"

But Portia stopped him, saying: "Softly; there is no haste. The Jew shall have nothing but the penalty. Therefore prepare, Shylock, to cut off the flesh; but mind you shed no blood; nor do not cut off more nor less than just a pound; be it more or less by one poor scruple[53], nay, if the scale turn but by the weight of a single hair, you are condemned[54] by the laws of Venice to die, and all your wealth is forfeited to the senate."

"Give me my money and let me go," said Shylock.

"I have it ready," said Bassanio. "Here it is."

Shylock was going to take the money, when Portia again stopped him, saying: "Tarry, Jew. I have yet another hold upon you. By the laws of Venice, your wealth is forfeited to the state for having conspired[55] against the life of one of its citizens, and your life lies at the mercy of the duke; therefore, down on your knees and ask him to pardon you."

---

53 scruple ['skruːpəl] (n.) 重量單位（等於 20 釐）
54 condemn [kən'dem] (v.) 判罪；處刑
55 conspire [kən'spaɪr] (v.) 密謀；陰謀

24   The duke then said to Shylock: "That you may see the difference of our Christian spirit, I pardon you your life before you ask it. Half your wealth belongs to Antonio, the other half comes to the state."

The generous Antonio then said that he would give up his share of Shylock's wealth, if Shylock would sign a deed to make it over at his death to his daughter and her husband; for Antonio knew that the Jew had an only daughter who had lately married against his consent to a young Christian named Lorenzo, a friend of Antonio's, which had so offended Shylock that he had disinherited her.

**25** The Jew agreed to this; and being thus disappointed in his revenge and despoiled[56] of his riches, he said: "I am ill. Let me go home. Send the deed after me, and I will sign over half my riches to my daughter."

"Get thee gone, then," said the duke, "and sign it; and if you repent[57] your cruelty and turn Christian, the state will forgive you the fine of the other half of your riches."

The duke now released Antonio and dismissed the court. He then highly praised the wisdom and ingenuity[58] of the young counselor and invited him home to dinner.

Portia, who meant to return to Belmont before her husband, replied, "I humbly thank your grace, but I must away directly."

The duke said he was sorry he had not leisure to stay and dine with him, and, turning to Antonio, he added, "Reward this gentleman; for in my mind you are much indebted to him."

---

56 despoil [dɪ'spɔɪl] (v.) 奪取；掠奪
57 repent [rɪ'pent] (v.) 悔悟；痛悔
58 ingenuity [ˌɪndʒə'njuːəti] (n.) 靈巧；機靈

🎧26  The duke and his senators left the court; and then Bassanio said to Portia: "Most worthy gentleman, I and my friend Antonio have by your wisdom been this day acquitted[59] of grievous penalties, and I beg you will accept of the three thousand ducats due unto the Jew."

"And we shall stand indebted to you over and above," said Antonio, "in love and service evermore."

Portia could not be prevailed[60] upon to accept the money. But upon Bassanio still pressing her to accept of some reward, she said: "Give me your gloves. I will wear them for your sake." And then Bassanio taking off his gloves, she espied[61] the ring which she had given him upon his finger. Now it was the ring the wily[62] lady wanted to get from him to make a merry jest when she saw her Bassanio again, that made her ask him for his gloves; and she said, when she saw the ring, "And for your love, I will take this ring from you."

---

59 acquit [əˈkwɪt] (v.) 宣告某人無罪
60 prevail [prɪˈveɪl] (v.) 勸導
61 espy [ɪsˈpaɪ] (v.) 看見；發現
62 wily [ˈwaɪli] (a.) 多智謀的；狡詐的

🎧 ⟨27⟩ Bassanio was sadly distressed that the counselor should ask him for the only thing he could not part with, and he replied, in great confusion, that he could not give him that ring, because it was his wife's gift and he had vowed never to part with it; but that he would give him the most valuable ring in Venice, and find it out by proclamation[63].

On this Portia affected to be affronted[64], and left the court, saying, "You teach me, sir, how a beggar should be answered."

"Dear Bassanio," said Antonio, "let him have the ring. Let My love and the great service he has done for me be valued against your wife's displeasure."

Bassanio, ashamed to appear so ungrateful, yielded, and sent Gratiano after Portia with the ring; and then the "clerk" Nerissa, who had also given Gratiano a ring, she begged his ring, and Gratiano (not choosing to be outdone in generosity by his lord) gave it to her.

And there was laughing among these ladies to think, when they got home, how they would tax[65] their husbands with giving away their rings and swear that they had given them as a present to some woman.

---

63 proclamation [ˌprɔːkləˈmeɪʃən] (n.) 宣告；公布
64 affront [əˈfrʌnt] (v.) 使當眾難堪
65 tax [tæks] (v.) 指控；責備

[28] Portia, when she returned, was in that happy temper of mind which never fails to attend the consciousness of having performed a good action. Her cheerful spirits enjoyed everything she saw: the moon never seemed to shine so bright before; and when that pleasant moon was hid behind a cloud, then a light which she saw from her house at Belmont as well pleased her charmed fancy, and she said to Nerissa: "That light we see is burning in my hall. How far that little candle throws its beams! So shines a good deed in a naughty world." And hearing the sound of music from her house, she said, "Methinks that music sounds much sweeter than by day."

And now Portia and Nerissa entered the house, and, dressing themselves in their own apparel, they awaited the arrival of their husbands, who soon followed them with Antonio; and Bassanio presenting his dear friend to the Lady Portia, the congratulations and welcomings of that lady were hardly over when they perceived Nerissa and her husband quarreling in a corner of the room.

"A quarrel already?" said Portia. "What is the matter?"

Gratiano replied, "Lady, it is about a paltry[66] gilt[67] ring that Nerissa gave me, with words upon it like the poetry on a cutler's[68] knife: '*Love me, and leave me not.*'"

"What does the poetry or the value of the ring signify?" said Nerissa. "You swore to me when I gave it to you, that you would keep it till the hour of death; and now you say you gave it to the lawyer's clerk. I know you gave it to a woman."

"By this hand," replied Gratiano, "I gave it to a youth, a kind of boy, a little scrubbed[69] boy, no higher than yourself; he was clerk to the young counselor that by his wise pleading saved Antonio's life. This prating[70] boy begged it for a fee, and I could not for my life deny him."

---

66 paltry ['pɔːltri] (a.) 無價值的；微不足道的
67 gilt [gɪlt] (n.) 鍍金材料
68 cutler ['kʌtlər] (n.) 刀匠
69 scrubbed [skrʌbd] (a.) 矮小的
70 prating ['preɪtɪŋ] (a.) 喋喋不休的

🎧 ⟨30⟩ Portia said: "You were to blame, Gratiano, to part with your wife's first gift. I gave my Lord Bassanio a ring, and I am sure he would not part with it for all the world."

Gratiano, in excuse for his fault, now said, "My Lord Bassanio gave his ring away to the counselor, and then the boy, his clerk, that took some pains in writing, he begged my ring."

Portia, hearing this, seemed very angry and reproached Bassanio for giving away her ring; and she said Nerissa had taught her what to believe, and that she knew some woman had the ring. Bassanio was very unhappy to have so offended his dear lady, and he said with great earnestness:

"No, by my honor, no woman had it, but a civil doctor who refused three thousand ducats of me and begged the ring, which when I denied him, he went displeased away. What could I do, sweet Portia? I was so beset[71] with shame for my seeming ingratitude that I was forced to send the ring after him. Pardon me, good lady. Had you been there, I think you would have begged the ring of me to give the worthy doctor."

"Ah!" said Antonio, "I am the unhappy cause of these quarrels."

71 beset [bɪˈsɛt] (v.) 包圍

BASSANIO.   By heaven, it is the same I gave the doctor!
PORTIA.        I had it of him: pardon me, Bassanio.

🎧 **31**     Portia bid Antonio not to grieve at that, for that he was welcome notwithstanding; and then Antonio said: "I once did lend my body for Bassanio's sake; and but for him to whom your husband gave the ring, I should have now been dead. I dare be bound again, my soul upon the forfeit, your lord will never more break his faith with you."

"Then you shall be his surety[72]," said Portia. "Give him this ring and bid him keep it better than the other."

When Bassanio looked at this ring, he was strangely surprised to find it was the same he gave away; and then Portia told him how she was the young counselor, and Nerissa was her clerk; and Bassanio found, to his unspeakable wonder and delight, that it was by the noble courage and wisdom of his wife that Antonio's life was saved.

And Portia again welcomed Antonio, and gave him letters which by some chance had fallen into her hands, which contained an account of Antonio's ships, that were supposed lost, being safely arrived in the harbor.

---

[72] surety [ˈsuəti] (n.) 保證人

32   So these tragical beginnings of this rich merchant's story were all forgotten in the unexpected good fortune which ensued[73]; and there was leisure to laugh at the comical adventure of the rings, and the husbands that did not know their own wives, Gratiano merrily swearing, in a sort of rhyming speech, that—

> *While he lived, he'd fear no other thing*
> *So sore, as keeping safe Nerissa's ring.*

73 ensue [ɪn'suː] (v.) 隨之發生

## Quotation
## The Merchant of Venice

**Shylock**
Go to then, you come to me, and you say,
"Shylock, we would have moneys." You say so...
Shall I bend low and in a bondman's key,
With bated breath and whispering humbleness,
Say this:
"Fair sir, you spit on me Wednesday last,
You spurn'd me such a day, another time
You call'd me dog; and for these courtesies
I'll lend you thus much moneys?"
(I, iii, 115-16, 123-29)

賽拉客
於是,您跑來找我,您說,
「賽拉客,我們要幾個錢。」您說了⋯⋯
我該不該哈著腰,像個奴才
低聲下氣恭恭敬敬地,說道:
「可愛的先生,您上星期三吐我口水,
還有一天您用腳踢我,另外一次
您喊我狗;為了報答這些厚愛,
所以我應該借給您這麼多錢?」
(第一幕,第三景,115-16 行,123-29 行)

**Portia**    The quality of mercy is not strain'd,
It droppeth as the gentle rain from heaven
Upon the place beneath. It is twice blest:
It blesseth him that gives and him that takes.
  (IV, i, 184-87)

波兒榭    仁慈非出自於勉強，
它如甘霖從天而降；
仁慈是雙重的福份，
施主和受者都賜福。
（第四幕，第一景，184-87 行）

---

**Shylock**    Most learned judge, a sentence! Come prepare!
**Portia**    Tarry a little, there is something else.
This bond doth give thee here no jot of blood;
The words expressly are "a pound of flesh."
(IV, i, 304-7)

賽拉客    博學多識的法官！判得好！來，準備了！
波兒榭    且慢，尚有一事。
約上未允諾給你血，
僅寫明「一磅肉」。
（第四幕，第一景，304-7 行）

# The Comedy of Errors

# 連環錯

# 導讀

## 故事架構與來源

《連環錯》約於 1593-94 年間完成，是莎劇中最短的一部。因為完成的年代最早，所以風格與架構最接近古典喜劇。這齣早期的喜劇，並為後來主題相似但技巧更為成熟的《第十二夜》奠定了基礎。

《連環錯》這整個故事都發生在同一天，發生的地點也在同一個地方，主要的情節則在身分錯認一事上，吻合古典戲劇理論中的「三一律」。莎劇少見合乎三一律的架構，除本劇之外，亦見於《暴風雨》。

《連環錯》應是根據羅馬喜劇作家普勞特斯（Plautus, 254?-184 B.C.）一齣典型孿生喜劇 Menaechmi 的故事大綱改編而成，華納（William Warner）以生動鮮活筆觸將其譯為英文，於 1595 年出版。部分學者認為《連環錯》之所以早一步問世，應該是由於莎士比亞看過拉丁原文或英譯本的初稿。

Menaechmi 描述一對雙胞胎兄弟在嬰兒時期分離，長大後在一個城鎮出現。這對孿生兄弟不時遭到誤認，不但令別人惱怒，兩個當事人也感到離奇困惑，一直到劇終兩人相見相認後才水落石出。《連環錯》與 Menaechmi 的相同之處在於：這些接踵而來的誤會都是由一連串的巧合機運所造成，並非人為的詭計或玩笑。

T. D. SCOTT.

G. GREATBACH.

但莎士比亞除了師法普勞特斯沿用原有的架構之外，又更勝一籌，加入一對孿生奴僕，並且取了相同的名字，使得原本就複雜的誤會，更是糾結難解。

此外，他還借用普勞特斯另一個劇本 Amphitruo 中的情節，寫下了雅卓安娜將丈夫關在門外，與她認定的丈夫在家裡用餐的這一景。兩兄弟的父親葉吉這個角色也不是莎士比亞所原創的，而是取材於十四世紀的詩人高爾（John Gower）所寫的《Appolonius of Tyre》。

孿生兄弟重逢的地點，由掖披丹改為以巫術著稱的以弗所（Ephesus），為小安提弗將誤會解釋為巫術的聯想，提供了絕佳的背景和笑點。此外，葉吉得以在劇終擺脫死刑的威脅，最後闔家團圓，與 Menaechmi 嘲諷式的賣妻結局大相逕庭，這也是莎士比亞的主意。

## 「笑劇」

儘管本劇是莎劇劇名中唯一中帶有喜劇（comedy）一詞的戲，但長久以來，許多評論家卻堅持這是齣笑劇（farce），不值得從喜劇的角度認真看待。英國詩人及評論家柯立芝（Samuel Taylor Coleridge）就曾經說過，雙胞胎的角色勉強維持了喜劇的主題，但增加另一對雙胞胎卻是劇作家與觀眾雙方同意的協定：即使是最誇張的機緣巧合，也可以在劇場中成立。

劇中的某些情節也具有笑劇的特徵，例如兩人闊別多年後竟會在同一天穿上一模一樣的服裝，又例如被誤認的孿生子毆打僕人，被認為精神錯亂，而他則將誤會都歸咎於巫術。《牛津英語大辭典》中為笑劇所下的定義是：

通常為篇幅較短的戲劇作品，以引人發笑為唯一的目的。

《連環錯》並不完全符合這個定義，因為劇中也有感人的情節，例如葉吉與雙胞胎兒子失散的苦難，男女的情愛，還有葉吉在最需要幫助時，親生兒子卻不認他。

更重要的是，莎士比亞使葉吉籠罩在死亡的陰影下，直到劇終才得以解除，而死亡在多數的羅馬喜劇中向來都只是虛晃一招，並沒有成真的可能。

席德尼爵士（Sir Philip Sidney）也說：「喜劇就是模仿生活中的誤會，用最滑稽可笑的方式呈現，使觀眾認為絕對不可能發生。」從這兩個角度來看，稱《連環錯》為喜劇並不為過。莎士比亞似乎在他早期的劇場生涯就已經認為：歷經一連串的道德衝突或生命危險之後，達到圓滿結局，才算是喜劇收場。

## 宗教意喻

其實在羅馬喜劇的背後，隱約還帶有希臘風格。西元前四世紀末希臘新喜劇（New Comedy）的創始人米南德（Menander, 342-292 B.C.）及其他劇作家，似乎都最鍾愛錯認身分、和失散子女重逢等主題，或許是因為當時的政治經濟狀況混亂，使得和小孩離散成為司空見慣的事件。

隨著時空的推移，經過羅馬時期到伊莉莎白時期，莎士比亞又賦予這個傳統的戲劇文類新的活力與意義，並加入了基督教對大眾心理及道德價值的影響。

《連環錯》的場景設在《聖經》中聖保羅與使徒前往的以弗所一地，藉此將基督教思想注入劇本，呼應劇中人物的情緒及心理反應。如葉吉最後出乎意料地無償獲得寬恕釋放就是最好的例子，其他類似的情節還反映在女修道院長是基督徒的典範，而劇中對婚姻的描述建立在互愛與互敬之上，同樣也吻合基督教的思想。

雅卓安娜潑悍是因為懷疑丈夫不愛她，丈夫又因為妻子和另一名男子一起吃飯，憤而去找其他女子，而露希安娜則認為為人妻子應順從丈夫才是正道，其語氣和思想都類似莎士比亞同時期的喜劇《馴悍記》中改頭換面的凱薩琳，代表基督教對婚姻的典型觀點。

## 各種主題

劇中人視周遭的人事物為理所當然，結果經由身分的錯置，使得他們能跳脫出原有觀點，重新審視生活中的大小事件。又待所有的混亂和誤解解除後，才恢復原有的秩序與理性，所有人生活回歸正常。其間的對比，如幻象與現實、瘋狂與理智，也是常見的莎劇主題。

在此劇，莎劇的另一個常見主題也有著墨：社會地位不平等的問題。一介平凡的商人無奈接受死刑，僕人遭主人毆打，諸如此類等等，都體現出此一問題。而在本劇中，作者並沒有允諾任何平等公義的力量，只展現出這種問題可以獲得解決，但本質仍然是無法改變的。

《連環錯》最早的演出紀錄是在 1594 年 12 月 28 日，當時正值聖誕假期。三百年後，波爾（William Poel）將此劇重新搬上葛雷法律學院的場地，旨在重現當時演出的風貌。這次演出讓人不得不承認《連環錯》在舞台上的確具有一定的戲劇效果，從此打破以往認為此劇過於粗俗、前後不相連貫的成見。時至今日，這齣戲仍然能夠引起許多觀眾（尤其是孩童）的笑聲及掌聲。

# 人物表

| Aegeon | 葉吉 | 溪洛窟的一位老商人 |
| --- | --- | --- |
| Antipholus | 安提弗 | 葉吉的雙胞胎兒子，兄弟同名 |
| Dromio | 拙米歐 | 孿生奴僕，兄弟同名 |
| Menaphon | 梅納封公爵 | 以弗所的安提弗的養父 |
| Adriana | 雅卓安娜 | 以弗所的安提弗的妻子 |
| Luciana | 露希安娜 | 雅卓安娜的妹妹 |
| lady abbess | 修道院院長 | 葉吉失散多年的妻子 |

🎧 (33) The states of Syracuse and Ephesus being at variance[1], there was a cruel law made at Ephesus, ordaining[2] that if any merchant of Syracuse was seen in the city of Ephesus, he was to be put to death, unless he could pay a thousand marks for the ransom[3] of his life.

Aegeon, an old merchant of Syracuse, was discovered in the streets of Ephesus, and brought before the duke, either to pay this heavy fine or to receive sentence of death.

Aegeon had no money to pay the fine, and the duke, before he pronounced the sentence of death upon him, desired him to relate the history of his life, and to tell for what cause he had ventured to come to the city of Ephesus, which it was death for any Syracusan merchant to enter.

Aegeon said that he did not fear to die, for sorrow had made him weary of his life, but that a heavier task could not have been imposed[4] upon him than to relate the events of his unfortunate life. He then began his own history, in the following words:

1 variance [ˈverɪəns] (n.) 意見不合；齟齬
2 ordain [ɔːrˈdeɪn] (v.) 命令；注定
3 ransom [ˈrænsəm] (n.) 贖金；贖回
4 impose [ɪmˈpoʊz] (v.) 徵……；加於

🎧 34 "I was born at Syracuse, and brought up to the profession of a merchant. I married a lady, with whom I lived very happily, but, being obliged to go to Epidamnum, I was detained there by my business six months, and then, finding I should be obliged to stay some time longer, I sent for my wife, who, as soon as she arrived, was brought to bed of two sons, and what was very strange, they were both so exactly alike that it was impossible to distinguish the one from the other.

"At the same time that my wife was brought to bed of these twin boys, a poor woman in the inn where my wife lodged was brought to bed of two sons, and these twins were as much like each other as my two sons were. The parents of these children being exceeding poor, I bought the two boys and brought them up to attend upon my sons.

Aegeon. A joyful mother of two goodly sons.

35 "My sons were very fine children, and my wife was not a little proud of two such boys; and she daily wishing to return home, I unwillingly agreed, and in an evil hour we got on shipboard, for we had not sailed above a league from Epidamnum before a dreadful storm arose, which continued with such violence that the sailors, seeing no chance of saving the ship, crowded into the boat to save their own lives, leaving us alone in the ship, which we every moment expected would be destroyed by the fury of the storm.

🎧 **36**     "The incessant[5] weeping of my wife and the piteous complaints of the pretty babes, who, not knowing what to fear, wept for fashion, because they saw their mother weep, filled me with terror for them, though I did not for myself fear death; and all my thoughts were bent to contrive[6] means for their safety. I tied my youngest son to the end of a small spare mast, such as seafaring men provide against storms; at the other end I bound the youngest of the twin slaves, and at the same time I directed my wife how to fasten the other children in like manner to another mast.

"She thus having the care of the two eldest children, and I of the two younger, we bound ourselves separately to these masts with the children; and but for this contrivance we had all been lost, for the ship split on a mighty rock and was dashed in pieces; and we, clinging to these slender masts, were supported above the water, where I, having the care of two children, was unable to assist my wife, who, with the other children, was soon separated from me; but while they were yet in my sight, they were taken up by a boat of fishermen, from Corinth (as I supposed), and, seeing them in safety.

---

5 incessant [ɪn'sesənt] (a.) 不斷的；不停的
6 contrive [kən'traɪv] (v.) 設計；想辦法

"I had no care but to struggle with the wild sea-waves, to preserve my dear son and the youngest slave. At length we, in our turn, were taken up by a ship, and the sailors, knowing me, gave us kind welcome and assistance and landed us in safety at Syracuse; but from that sad hour I have never known what became of my wife and eldest child.

"My youngest son, and now my only care, when he was eighteen years of age, began to be inquisitive[7] after his mother and his brother, and often importuned[8] me that he might take his attendant, the young slave, who had also lost his brother, and go in search of them. At length I unwillingly gave consent, for, though I anxiously desired to hear tidings of my wife and eldest son, yet in sending my younger one to find them, I hazarded the loss of him also.

7 inquisitive [ɪnˈkwɪzɪtɪv] (a.) 好管閒事的
8 importune [ˌɪmpərˈtuːn] (v.) 再三請求

"It is now seven years since my son left me; five years have I passed in traveling through the world in search of him. I have been in farthest Greece, and through the bounds of Asia, and, coasting homewards, I landed here in Ephesus, being unwilling to leave any place unsought that harbors men; but this day must end the story of my life, and happy should I think myself in my death if I were assured my wife and sons were living."

Here the hapless[9] Aegeon ended the account of his misfortunes; and the duke, pitying this unfortunate father who had brought upon himself this great peril by his love for his lost son, said if it were not against the laws, which his oath and dignity did not permit him to alter, he would freely pardon him; yet, instead of dooming him to instant death, as the strict letter of the law required, he would give him that day to try if he could beg or borrow the money to pay the fine.

9 hapless ['hæpləs] (a.) 不幸的

🎧 **39**     This day of grace did seem no great favor to Aegeon, for, not knowing any man in Ephesus, there seemed to him but little chance that any stranger would lend or give him a thousand marks to pay the fine; and, helpless and hopeless of any relief, he retired from the presence of the duke in the custody[10] of a jailor.

Aegeon supposed he knew no person in Ephesus; but at the very time he was in danger of losing his life through the careful search he was making after his youngest son, that son, and his eldest son also, were both in the city of Ephesus.

---

10 custody [ˈkʌstədi] (n.) 監禁

🎧 **40** Aegeon's sons, besides being exactly alike in face and person, were both named alike, being both called Antipholus, and the two twin slaves were also both named Dromio. Aegeon's youngest son, Antipholus of Syracuse, he whom the old man had come to Ephesus to seek, happened to arrive at Ephesus with his slave Dromio that very same day that Aegeon did; and he being also a merchant of Syracuse, he would have been in the same danger that his father was, but by good fortune he met a friend who told him the peril an old merchant of Syracuse was in, and advised him to pass for a merchant of Epidamnum. This Antipholus agreed to do, and he was sorry to hear one of his own countrymen was in this danger, but he little thought this old merchant was his own father.

🎧 The eldest son of Aegeon (who must be called Antipholus of Ephesus, to distinguish him from his brother Antipholus of Syracuse) had lived at Ephesus twenty years, and, being a rich man, was well able to have paid the money for the ransom of his father's life; but Antipholus knew nothing of his father, being so young when he was taken out of the sea with his mother by the fishermen that he only remembered he had been so preserved; but he had no recollection of either his father or his mother, the fishermen who took up this Antipholus and his mother and the young slave Dromio, having carried the two children away from her (to the great grief of that unhappy lady), intending to sell them.

Antipholus and Dromio were sold by them to Duke Menaphon, a famous warrior, who was uncle to the Duke of Ephesus, and he carried the boys to Ephesus when he went to visit the duke, his nephew.

 The Duke of Ephesus, taking a liking to young Antipholus, when he grew up, made him an officer in his army, in which he distinguished himself by his great bravery in the wars, where he saved the life of his patron, the duke, who rewarded his merit by marrying him to Adriana, a rich lady of Ephesus, with whom he was living (his slave Dromio still attending him) at the time his father came there.

Antipholus of Syracuse, when he parted with his friend, who, advised him to say he came from Epidamnum, gave his slave Dromio some money to carry to the inn where he intended to dine, and in the mean time he said he would walk about and view the city and observe the manners of the people.

Go bear it to the Centaur, where we host,          Act. 1  Scene. 2
And stay there, Dromio, till I come to thee.

**(43)**   Dromio was a pleasant fellow, and when Antipholus was dull and melancholy he used to divert[11] himself with the odd humors and merry jests of his slave, so that the freedoms of speech he allowed in Dromio were greater than is usual between masters and their servants.

When Antipholus of Syracuse had sent Dromio away, he stood awhile thinking over his solitary[12] wanderings in search of his mother and his brother, of whom in no place where he landed could he hear the least tidings; and he said sorrowfully to himself, "I am like a drop of water in the ocean, which, seeking to find its fellow drop, loses itself in the wide sea. So I, unhappily, to find a mother and a brother, do lose myself."

---

11 divert [daɪ'vɜːrt] (v.) 娛樂；款待
12 solitary ['sɔːləteri] (a.) 單獨的

While he was thus meditating on his weary travels, which had hitherto been so useless, Dromio (as he thought) returned. Antipholus, wondering that he came back so soon, asked him where he had left the money. Now it was not his own Dromio, but the twin-brother that lived with Antipholus of Ephesus, that he spoke to. The two Dromios and the two Antipholuses were still as much alike as Aegeon had said they were in their infancy[13]; therefore no wonder Antipholus thought it was his own slave returned, and asked him why he came back so soon.

Dromio replied: "My mistress sent me to bid you come to dinner. The capon[14] burns, and the pig falls from the spit[15], and the meat will be all cold if you do not come home."

"These jests are out of season," said Antipholus. "Where did you leave the money?"

"Dromio still answering that his mistress had sent him to fetch Antipholus to dinner, "What mistress?" said Antipholus.

---

13 infancy ['ɪnfənsi] (n.) 嬰兒期;幼兒
14 capon ['keɪpən] (n.) 閹雞
15 spit [spɪt] (n.) 烤肉叉

"Why, your worship's wife, sir!" replied Dromio.

Antipholus having no wife, he was very angry with Dromio, and said: "Because I familiarly sometimes chat with you, you presume[16] to jest with me in this free manner. I am not in a sportive humor now. Where is the money? We being strangers here, how dare you trust so great a charge from your own custody?"

Dromio, hearing his master, as he thought him, talk of their being strangers, supposing Antipholus was jesting, replied, merrily: "I pray you, sir, jest as you sit at dinner. I had no charge but to fetch you home to dine with my mistress and her sister."

Now Antipholus lost all patience, and beat Dromio, who ran home and told his mistress that his master had refused to come to dinner and said that he had no wife.

16 presume [prɪˈzuːm] (v.) 擅敢；冒昧

🎧 46    Adriana, the wife of Antipholus of Ephesus, was very angry when she heard that her husband said he had no wife; for she was of a jealous temper, and she said her husband meant that he loved another lady better than herself; and she began to fret[17], and say unkind words of jealousy and reproach of her husband; and her sister Luciana, who lived with her, tried in vain to persuade her out of her groundless suspicions.

Antipholus of Syracuse went to the inn, and found Dromio with the money in safety there, and, seeing his own Dromio, he was going again to chide[18] him for his free jests, when Adriana came up to him, and, not doubting but it was her husband she saw, she began to reproach him for looking strange upon her (as well he might, never having seen this angry lady before); and then she told him how well he loved her before they were married, and that now he loved some other lady instead of her.

"How comes it now, my husband," said she, "oh, how comes it that I have lost your love?"

"Plead you to me, fair dame?" said the astonished Antipholus.

---

17 fret [frɛt] (v.) 煩惱；不滿；煩躁
18 chide [tʃaɪd] (v.) 責怪；斥責

It was in vain he told her he was not her husband and that he had been in Ephesus but two hours. She insisted on his going home with her, and Antipholus at last, being unable to get away, went with her to his brother's house, and dined with Adriana and her sister, the one calling him husband and the other brother, he, all amazed, thinking he must have been married to her in his sleep, or that he was sleeping now. And Dromio, who followed them, was no less surprised, for the cook-maid, who was his brother's wife, also claimed him for her husband.

While Antipholus of Syracuse was dining with his brother's wife, his brother, the real husband, returned home to dinner with his slave Dromio; but the servants would not open the door, because their mistress had ordered them not to admit any company; and when they repeatedly knocked, and said they were Antipholus and Dromio, the maids laughed at them, and said that Antipholus was at dinner with their mistress, and Dromio was in the kitchen, and though they almost knocked the door down, they could not gain admittance, and at last Antipholus went away very angry, and strangely surprised at, hearing a gentleman was dining with his wife.

🎧 48 When Antipholus of Syracuse had finished his dinner, he was so perplexed[19] at the lady's still persisting in calling him husband, and at hearing that Dromio had also been claimed by the cookmaid, that he left the house as soon as he could find any pretence[20] to get away; for though he was very much pleased with Luciana, the sister, yet the jealous-tempered Adriana he disliked very much, nor was Dromio at all better satisfied with his fair wife in the kitchen; therefore both master and man were glad to get away from their new wives as fast as they could.

The moment Antipholus of Syracuse had left the house he was met by a goldsmith, who, mistaking him, as Adriana had done, for Antipholus of Ephesus, gave him a gold chain, calling him by his name; and when Antipholus would have refused the chain, saying it did not belong to him, the goldsmith replied he made it by his own orders, and went away, leaving the chain in the hands of Antipholus, who ordered his man Dromio to get his things on board a ship, not choosing to stay in a place any longer where he met with such strange adventures that he surely thought himself bewitched[21].

---

19 perplexed [pər'plɛkst] (a.) 困惑的
20 pretence ['priːtens] (n.) 藉口；託辭
21 bewitched [bɪ'wɪtʃt] (a.) 中邪的

🎧 49  The goldsmith who had given the chain to the wrong Antipholus was arrested immediately after for a sum of money he owed; and Antipholus, the married brother, to whom the goldsmith thought he had given the chain, happened to come to the place where the officer was arresting the goldsmith, who, when he saw Antipholus, asked him to pay for the gold chain he had just delivered to him, the price amounting to nearly the same sum as that for which he had been arrested.

Antipholus denying the having received the chain, and the goldsmith persisting to declare that he had but a few minutes before given it to him, they disputed this matter a long time, both thinking they were right; for Antipholus knew the goldsmith never gave him the chain, and so like were the two brothers, the goldsmith was as certain he had delivered the chain into his hands, till at last the officer took the goldsmith away to prison for the debt he owed, and at the same time the goldsmith made the officer arrest Antipholus for the price of the chain; so that at the conclusion of their dispute, Antipholus and the merchant were both taken away to prison together.

🎧50  As Antipholus was going to prison, he met Dromio of Syracuse, his brother's slave, and, mistaking him for his own, he ordered him to go to Adriana his wife, and tell her to send the money for which he was arrested.

Dromio, wondering that his master should send him back to the strange house where he dined, and from which he had just before been in such haste to depart, did not dare to reply, though he came to tell his master the ship was ready to sail, for he saw Antipholus was in no humor to be jested with. Therefore he went away, grumbling within himself that he must return to Adriana's house, "Where," said he, "Dowsabel claims me for a husband. But I must go, for servants must obey their masters' commands."

Adriana gave him the money, and as Dromio was returning he met Antipholus of Syracuse, who was still in amaze at the surprising adventures he met with, for his brother being well known in Ephesus, there was hardly a man he met in the streets but saluted him as an old acquaintance. Some offered him money which they said was owing to him, some invited him to come and see them, and some gave him thanks for kindnesses they said he had done them, all mistaking him for his brother. A tailor showed him some silks he had bought for him, and insisted upon taking measure of him for some clothes.

🎧 51　　Antipholus began to think he was among a nation of sorcerers[22] and witches, and Dromio did not at all relieve his master from his bewildered[23] thoughts by asking him how he got free from the officer who was carrying him to prison, and giving him the purse of gold which Adriana had sent to pay the debt with.

　　This talk of Dromio's of the arrest and of a prison, and of the money he had brought from Adriana, perfectly confounded Antipholus, and he said, "This fellow Dromio is certainly distracted[24], and we wander here in illusions," and, quite terrified at his own confused thoughts, he cried out, "Some blessed power deliver us from this strange place!"

　　And now another stranger came up to him, and she was a lady, and she, too, called him Antipholus, and told him he had dined with her that day, and asked him for a gold chain which she said he had promised to give her.

---

22 sorcerer ['sɔːrsərər] (n.) 魔法師；術士；男巫師
23 bewildered [bɪ'wɪldərd] (a.) 迷惑的；中邪的
24 distracted [dɪ'stræktɪd] (a.) 心情紛亂的

🎧 52    Antipholus now lost all patience, and, calling her a sorceress, he denied that he had ever promised her a chain, or dined with her, or had even seen her face before that moment. The lady persisted in affirming he had dined with her and had promised her a chain, which Antipholus still denying, she further said that she had given him a valuable ring, and if he would not give her the gold chain, she insisted upon having her own ring again.

On this Antipholus became quite frantic[25], and again calling her sorceress and witch, and denying all knowledge of her or her ring, ran away from her, leaving her astonished at his words and his wild looks, for nothing to her appeared more certain than that he had dined with her, and that she had given him a ring in consequence of his promising to make her a present of a gold chain. But this lady had fallen into the same mistake the others had done, for she had taken him for his brother; the married Antipholus had done all the things she taxed this Antipholus with.

25 frantic ['fræntɪk] (a.) 狂亂的

When the married Antipholus was denied entrance into his house (those within supposing him to be already there), he had gone away very angry, believing it to be one of his wife's jealous freaks, to which she was very subject, and, remembering that she had often falsely accused him of visiting other ladies, he, to be revenged on her for shutting him out of his own house, determined to go and dine with this lady, and she receiving him with great civility, and his wife having so highly offended him, Antipholus promised to give her a gold chain which he had intended as a present for his wife; it was the same chain which the goldsmith by mistake had given to his brother.

The lady liked so well the thoughts of having a fine gold chain that she gave the married Antipholus a ring; which when, as she supposed (taking his brother for him), he denied, and said he did not know her, and left her in such a wild passion, she began to think he was certainly out of his senses; and presently she resolved to go and tell Adriana that her husband was mad.

54 And while she was telling it to Adriana, he came, attended by the jailor (who allowed him to come home to get the money to pay the debt), for the purse of money which Adriana had sent by Dromio and he had delivered to the other Antipholus.

Adriana believed the story the lady told her of her husband's madness must be true when he reproached her for shutting him out of his own house; and remembering how he had protested all dinner-time that he was not her husband and had never been in Ephesus till that day, she had no doubt that he was mad; she therefore paid the jailor the money, and, having discharged him, she ordered her servants to bind her husband with ropes, and had him conveyed into a dark room, and sent for a doctor to come and cure him of his madness, Antipholus all the while hotly exclaiming against this false accusation, which the exact likeness he bore to his brother had brought upon him. But his rage only the more confirmed them in the belief that he was mad; and Dromio persisting in the same story, they bound him also and took him away along with his master.

55   Soon after Adriana had put her husband into confinement[26] a servant came to tell her that Antipholus and Dromio must have broken loose from their keepers, for that they were both walking at liberty in the next street.

On hearing this, Adriana ran out to fetch him home, taking some people with her to secure her husband again; and her sister went along with her.

When they came to the gates of a convent[27] in their neighborhood, there they saw Antipholus and Dromio, as they thought, being again deceived by the likeness of the twin brothers.

Antipholus of Syracuse was still beset with the perplexities this likeness had brought upon him. The chain which the goldsmith had given him was about his neck, and the goldsmith was reproaching him for denying that he had it and refusing to pay for it, and Antipholus was protesting that the goldsmith freely gave him the chain in the morning, and that from that hour he had never seen the goldsmith again.

---

26 confinement [kən'faɪnmənt] (n.) 限制；監禁
27 convent ['kɑːnvənt] (n.) 女修道院

## 56

And now Adriana came up to him and claimed him as her lunatic husband who had escaped from his keepers, and the men she brought with her were going to lay violent hands on Antipholus and Dromio; but they ran into the convent, and Antipholus begged the abbess[28] to give him shelter in her house.

And now came out the lady abbess herself to inquire into the cause of this disturbance. She was a grave and venerable lady, and wise to judge of what she saw, and she would not too hastily give up the man who had sought protection in her house; so she strictly questioned the wife about the story she told of her husband's madness, and she said: "What is the cause of this sudden distemper[29] of your husband's? Has he lost his wealth at sea? Or is it the death of some dear friend that has disturbed his mind?"

Adriana replied that no such things as these had been the cause.

"Perhaps," said the abbess, "he has fixed his affections on some other lady than you, his wife, and that has driven him to this state."

28 abbess ['æbɪs] (n.) 女修道院院長
29 distemper [dɪ'stempər] (n.) 思緒混亂

## 57

Adriana said she had long thought the love of some other lady was the cause of his frequent absences from home.

Now it was not his love for another, but the teasing jealousy of his wife's temper, that often obliged Antipholus to leave his home; and the abbess (suspecting this from the vehemence[30] of Adriana's manner), to learn the truth, said: "You should have reprehended[31] him for this."

"Why, so I did," replied Adriana.

"Aye," said the abbess, "but perhaps not enough."

Adriana, willing to convince the abbess that she had said enough to Antipholus on this subject, replied: "It was the constant subject of our conversation; in bed I would not let him sleep for speaking of it. At table I would not let him eat for speaking of it. When I was alone with him I talked of nothing else; and in company I gave him frequent hints of it. Still all my talk was how vile[32] and bad it was in him to love any lady better than me."

---

30 vehemence ['viːməns] (n.) 猛烈
31 reprehend [ˌreprɪ'hend] (v.) 責難；譴責
32 vile [vaɪl] (a.) 卑鄙的

(58) The lady abbess, having drawn this full confession from the jealous Adriana, now said: "And therefore comes it that your husband is mad. The venomous[33] clamor[34] of a jealous woman is a more deadly poison than a mad dog's tooth. It seems his sleep was hindered by your railing; no wonder that his head is light; and his meat was sauced with your upbraidings[35]; unquiet meals make ill digestions, and that has thrown him into this fever. You say his sports were disturbed by your brawls[36]; being debarred[37] from the enjoyment of society and recreation, what could ensue but dull melancholy and comfortless despair? The consequence is, then, that your jealous fits have made your husband mad."

Luciana would have excused her sister, saying she always reprehended her husband mildly; and she said to her sister, "Why do you hear these rebukes[38] without answering them?"

33 venomous ['vɛnəməs] (a.) 惡毒的
34 clamor ['klæmər] (n.) 喧鬧
35 upbraiding [ʌp'breɪdɪŋ] (n.) 斥責；譴責
36 brawl [brɔːl] (n.) 大聲的爭吵
37 debar [dɪ'bɑːr] (v.) 排除
38 rebuke [rɪ'bjuːk] (n.) 指責

🎧 **59** But the abbess had made her so plainly perceive her fault that she could only answer, "She has betrayed me to my own reproof[39]."

Adriana, though ashamed of her own conduct, still insisted on having her husband delivered up to her; but the abbess would suffer no person to enter her house, nor would she deliver up this unhappy man to the care of the jealous wife, determining herself to use gentle means for his recovery, and she retired into her house again, and ordered her gates to be shut against them.

During the course of this eventful day, in which so many errors had happened from the likeness the twin brothers bore to each other, old Aegeon's day of grace was passing away, it being now near sunset; and at sunset he was doomed to die if he could not pay the money.

The place of his execution was near this convent, and here he arrived just as the abbess retired into the convent; the duke attending in person, that, if any offered to pay the money, he might be present to pardon him.

---

39 reproof [rɪˈpruːf] (n.) 譴責；非難

Adriana stopped this melancholy procession, and cried out to the duke for justice, telling him that the abbess had refused to deliver up her lunatic[40] husband to her care. While she was speaking, her real husband and his servant, Dromio, who had got loose, came before the duke to demand justice, complaining that his wife had confined him on a false charge of lunacy, and telling in what manner he had broken his bands and eluded[41] the vigilance[42] of his keepers.

40 lunatic ['luːnətɪk] (a.) 瘋的；精神錯亂的
41 elude [ɪ'luːd] (v.) 逃避
42 vigilance ['vɪdʒɪləns] (n.) 留心；警戒

Adriana was strangely surprised to see her husband when she thought he had been within the convent.

Aegeon, seeing his son, concluded this was the son who had left him to go in search of his mother and his brother, and he felt secure that this dear son would readily pay the money demanded for his ransom. He therefore spoke to Antipholus in words of fatherly affection, with joyful hope that he should now be released.

But, to the utter astonishment of Aegeon, his son denied all knowledge of him, as well he might, for this Antipholus had never seen his father since they were separated in the storm in his infancy. But while the poor old Aegeon was in vain endeavoring to make his son acknowledge him, thinking surely that either his griefs and the anxieties he had suffered had so strangely altered him that his son did not know him or else that he was ashamed to acknowledge his father in his misery— in the midst of this perplexity, the lady abbess and the other Antipholus and Dromio came out, and the wondering Adriana saw two husbands and two Dromios standing before her.

THE
COMEDY
OF
ERRORS.

ILLUS<sup>D</sup> BY C<sup>S</sup>                    T. COBB. S<sup>C</sup>

🎧62 And now these riddling errors, which had so perplexed them all, were clearly made out. When the duke saw the two Antipholuses and the two Dromios both so exactly alike, he at once conjectured[43] aright of these seeming mysteries, for he remembered the story Aegeon had told him in the morning; and he said these men must be the two sons of Aegeon and their twin slaves.

But now an unlooked-for joy indeed completed the history of Aegeon; and the tale he had in the morning told in sorrow, and under sentence of death, before the setting sun went down was brought to a happy conclusion, for the venerable lady abbess made herself known to be the long-lost wife of Aegeon and the fond mother of the two Antipholuses.

When the fishermen took the eldest Antipholus and Dromio away from her, she entered a nunnery, and by her wise and virtuous conduct she was at length made lady abbess of this convent and in discharging the rites of hospitality to an unhappy stranger she had unknowingly protected her own son.

43 conjecture [kənˈdʒektʃər] (v.) 推測；猜測

🎧 63 Joyful congratulations and affectionate greetings between these long-separated parents and their children made them for a while forget that Aegeon was yet under sentence of death. But when they were become a little calm, Antipholus of Ephesus offered the duke the ransom money for his father's life; but the duke freely pardoned Aegeon, and would not take the money.

And the duke went with the abbess and her newly found husband and children into the convent, to hear this happy family discourse at leisure of the blessed ending of their adverse[44] fortunes. And the two Dromios' humble joy must not be forgotten; they had their congratulations and greetings, too, and each Dromio pleasantly complimented his brother on his good looks, being well pleased to see his own person (as in a glass) show so handsome in his brother.

44 adverse ['ædvɜːrs] (a.) 不利的；反對的

🎧 **64**   Adriana had so well profited by the good counsel of her mother-in-law that she never after cherished unjust suspicions or was jealous of her husband.

Antipholus of Syracuse married the fair Luciana, the sister of his brother's wife; and the good old Aegeon, with his wife and sons, lived at Ephesus many years. Nor did the unraveling of these perplexities so entirely remove every ground of mistake for the future but that sometimes, to remind them of adventures past, comical blunders would happen, and the one Antipholus, and the one Dromio, be mistaken for the other, making altogether a pleasant and diverting Comedy of Errors.

# Quotation
## THE COMEDY OF ERRORS

| | |
|---|---|
| **Dromio** | But I pray, sir, why am I beaten? |
| **Antipholus** | Dost thou not know? |
| **Dromio** | Nothing, sir, but that I am beaten. |
| **Antipholus** | Shall I tell you why? |
| **Dromio** | Ay, sir, and wherefore; for they say, every why hath a wherefore. |
| **Antipholus** | Why, first, for flouting me, and then wherefore, for urging it the second time to me. |
| **Dromio** | Was there ever any man thus beaten out of season, When in the why and the wherefore is neither rhyme nor reason? |

(II, ii, 39-48)

| | |
|---|---|
| 拙米歐 | 少爺，我為什麼要挨打？ |
| 安提弗 | 你不知道嗎？ |
| 拙米歐 | 少爺，我不知道，我只知道我挨打了。 |
| 安提弗 | 要我告訴你理由嗎？ |
| 拙米歐 | 是，少爺，還有原因，因為俗話説得好，<br>理出必有因。 |
| 安提弗 | 先説理由，你頂撞我，再説原因，<br>還逼問我為什麼。 |
| 拙米歐 | 真倒楣，白白挨了這一頓拳腳，<br>理由和原因卻還是莫名其妙。 |

（第二幕，第二景，39-48 行）

國家圖書館出版品預行編目資料

悅讀莎士比亞故事 .6, 威尼斯商人 & 連環錯 / Charles and
Mary Lamb 著 ; Cosmos Language Workshop　譯 .
一初版 . 一 [ 臺北市 ] : 寂天文化，2012.5　面；公分 .

ISBN　978-986-184-955-3　(25K 平裝附光碟片 )

1. 英語 2. 讀本

805.18　　　　　　　　　　　　　　　　100025257

| | |
|---|---|
| 作者 | Charles and Mary Lamb |
| 譯者 | Cosmos Language Workshop |
| 編輯 | 蔡智堯 |
| 主編 | 黃鈺云 |
| 內文排版 | 陸葵珍 |
| 製程管理 | 蔡智堯 |
| 出版者 | 寂天文化事業股份有限公司 |
| 電話 | 02-2365-9739 |
| 傳真 | 02-2365-9835 |
| 網址 | www.icosmos.com.tw |
| 讀者服務 | onlineservice@icosmos.com.tw |
| 出版日期 | 2012 年 5 月 初版一刷（250101） |
| | 版權所有 請勿翻印 |
| 郵撥帳號 | 1998620-0 寂天文化事業股份有限公司 |
| | 訂購金額 600（含）元以上郵資免費 |
| | 訂購金額 600 元以下者，請外加郵資 60 元 |
| | 〔若有破損，請寄回更換，謝謝。〕 |

# CONTENTS

## 《威尼斯商人》Practice

### I Postreading

1. How did you think would the story end before you knew the outcome? What was your reaction when it comes to the end?

2. Do you sometimes live in an unaffordable luxury like Bassanio? If so, why?

### 2 Vocabulary: Fill in the blanks with appropriate words.

1. There was great e_____y between this c_____s Jew and the generous merchant Antonio.

2. If he did not repay the money by a certain day, he would f_____t a pound of flesh, to be cut off from any part of his body that Shylock pleased.

3. A pound of man's flesh, taken from a man, is not so e_____e, nor profitable neither, as the flesh of mutton or beef.

4. Bassanio being so kindly supplied with money by his friend Antonio, set out for Belmont with a s_____d train.

5. Bassanio begged the learned young counselor would e_____r to wrest the law a little, to save Antonio's life.

6. Antonio with a calm r_____n replied, that he had but little to say, for that he had prepared his mind for death.

7. By the laws of Venice, your wealth is forfeited to the state, for having c_____red against the life of one of its citizens.

8. The duke highly praised the wisdom and i_____y of the young counsellor, and invited him home to dinner.

9. Portia affected to be a_____ted, and left the court, saying: "You teach me, sir, how a beggar should be answered."

| Antonio | Bassanio | The Duke of Venice | Lorenzo |
| Gratiano | Nerissa | Portia | Shylock |

## A. Who are they?

1. _____ A rich heiress that Bassanio wished to marry, who, with her wonderful sagacity, delivered Antonio.

2. _____ A Jewish usurer who had amassed an immense fortune by lending money at great interest to Christian merchants.

3. _____ A young merchant of Venice, in whom the ancient Roman honor more appeared than in any that drew breath in Italy.

4. _____ A friend of Antonio's, to whom Shylock's only daughter had married and was disinherited.

5. _____ Bassanio's attendant, who loved to copy what his lord did.

6. _____ Antonio's nearest and dearest friend, who, having but a small patrimony, wished to marry a rich heiress whom he dearly loved.

## B. Who said these?

1. _____ "Shall I bend low and say, Fair sir, you spit upon me on Wednesday last, another time you called me dog, and for these courtesies I am to lend you monies."

2. _____ "If you will lend me this money, lend it not to me as to a friend, but rather lend it to me as to an enemy, that, if I break, you may with better face exact the penalty."

3. _____ "I am married to a wife, who is as dear to me as life itself; but life itself, my wife, and all the world, are not esteemed with me above your life."

4. _____ "Tarry a little, Jew, there is something else. This bond here gives you no drop of blood; the words expressly are 'a pound of flesh'."

5. _____ "That you may see the difference of our Christian spirit, I pardon you your life before you ask it."

6. _____ "It is about a paltry gilt ring that Nerissa gave me, with words upon it like the poetry on a cutler's knife; Love me, and leave me not."

7. _____ "You swore to me when I gave it to you, that you would keep it till the hour of death; and now you say you gave it to the lawyer's clerk. I know you gave it to a woman."

8. _____ "That light we see is burning in my hall; how far that little candle throws its beams, so shines a good deed in a naughty world."

---

**4**    **Comprehension: Choose the correct answer.**

____ 1. Why was Shylock much disliked by all good men, particularly by Antonio?
   a) Because he was a Jew.
   b) Because he was a hard-hearted usurer.
   c) Because he lived at Venice.
   d) Because he spit upon Antonio, and spurned at him with his foot.

____ 2. Why did Bassanio borrow three thousand ducats from Antonio?
   a) He had exhausted his little patrimony by living in too expensive a manner.
   b) He intended to prove that he and Antonio had but one heart and one purse between them.
   c) He wanted to furnish himself with an appearance befitting the lover of so rich an heiress.
   d) He wished to amass an immense fortune by borrowing money from his friends.

____ 3. How did Antonio lend Bassanio 3,000 ducats?
    a) He signed to a bond and procured it of Shylock.
    b) He ordered his ships to come home early laden
       with merchandise.
    c) He married a rich heiress who lived near Venice, at
       a place called Belmont.
    d) He sold his most valuable ring in Venice.

____ 4. What did Shylock exact from Antonio if he did not
    repay the money by a certain day?
    a) Twenty times of the money.
    b) His fair mansion all his servants.
    c) A ring he had vowed never to part with.
    d) A pound of his flesh.

____ 5. Who saved Antonio's life under the disguise of a
    counselor named Balthasar?
    a) Bassanio.               b) Bellario.
    c) The duke of Venice.    d) Portia.

____ 6. What did Portia do to speak in Antonio's defence in
    the trial?
    a) She spoke sweetly of the noble quality of mercy.
    b) She asked him to take the money Bassanio would
       repay him.
    c) She demanded him to cut off the pound of flesh
       without shedding any of Antonio's blood.
    d) All of the above.

____ 7. What was the cause of the quarrel between Portia
    and Bassanio?
    a) The 3,000 ducats.
    b) A ring.
    c) The argument between Gratiano and Nerissa.
    d) Antonio's visit.

____ 8. For what would Antonio give up his share of
    Shylock's wealth?
    a) If Shylock would quit usury.
    b) If Shylock would repent his cruelty and turn
       Christian.
    c) If Shylock would sign a deed to make it over at his
       death to his daughter and her husband.
    d) If Shylock would find all of Antonio's lost ships.

## 5 Discussion

1. Is Shylock an unforgivable villain? Why do you think he was so spiteful? Would you act likewise if you were treated the same way as he was?

2. Which do you value more—your lover or your best friend? What would you do if you faced the dilemma as Bassanio did?

3. Discuss the writing techniques in the story. How was the problem of "having a pound of flesh cut" created, led to the extreme tension, and then resolved?

## 6 Advise Bassanio

If Antonio did not lend Bassanio 3,000 ducats to propose to Portia, Shylock would never have the chance to set up this malicious plot. Suppose you are Bassanio's friend, try to dissuade him from borrowing the money from Antonio. Give convincing and persuasive reasons and supporting points.

## 7 What if . . .

The storyline of *The Merchant of Venice* goes as if on a tight rope. If an episode changes, the whole story would be quite different. Imagine any one of the following things happened, what do you think would become of the characters? Tell the rest of the story.

1. *Antonio would not lend the money to Bassanio.*

2. *Portia refused to marry Bassanio when she found him poor.*

3. *Shylock asked for Antonio's life in the bond.*

## 8 Promote the Production

The Merchant of Venice is made into a film. You are a copywriter, and you need to write several sentences to promote this film in a CF (commercial film), in magazines and in the poster on buses and MRT stations. What would you write in order to attract as many people as possible to go to the movie theatre?

## 《威尼斯商人》 Answers

### 2 Vocabulary
**A.**
1. enmity, covetous
2. forfeit
3. estimable
4. splendid
5. endeavour
6. resignation
7. conspired
8. ingenuity
9. affronted

### 3 Identification
**A.**
1. Portia
2. Shylock
3. Antonio
4. Lorenzo
5.Gratiano
6.Bassanio

**B.**
1. Shylock
2. Antonio
3. Bassanio
4. Portia
5. the duke of Venice
6. Gratiano
7. Nerissa
8. Portia

### 4 Comprehension
1. b
2. c
3. a
4. d
5. d
6. d
7. b
8. c

## 《連環錯》 Practice

**I Postreading**

Do you know any twins? Have you ever mistaken one of the twins for another? Tell us your experiences.

**2 Vocabulary: Fill in the blanks with appropriate words.**

1. If any merchant of Syracuse was seen in the city of Ephesus, he was to be put to death, unless he could pay a thousand marks for the r_____m of his life.

2. My youngest son often i_____ned me that he might take his attendant, the young slave, who had also lost his brother, and go in search of them.

3. He retired from the presence of the duke in the c_____y of a jailor.

4. He stood awhile thinking over his s_____y wanderings in search of his mother and his brother, of whom in no place where he landed could he hear the least tidings.

5. The two Dromios and the two Antipholuses were still as much alike as Aegeon had said they were in their i_____y.

6. He was perplexed at the lady's still p_____ting in calling him husband.

7. He met with such strange adventures in this place that he surely thought himself b_____hed.

8. This fellow Dromio is certainly distracted, and we wander here in i_____ns.

9. He had gone away very angry, believing it to be one of his wife's jealous f_____ks.

10. Adriana cried out to the duke for justice, telling him that the abbess had refused to deliver up her l_____c husband to her care.

**Identification**

**A. Draw a family tree of these characters.**

| | |
|---|---|
| a. Aegeon | b. the abbess |
| c. Antipholus of Ephesus | d. Dromio of Ephesus |
| e. Antipholus of Syracuse | f. Dromio of Syracuse |
| g. Adriana | h. Lucian |

**B. Who said these words?**

_____ 1. "The parents of these children being exceeding poor, I bought the two boys, and brought them up to attend upon my sons."

_____ 2. "I am like a drop of water in the ocean, which seeking to find its fellow drop, loses itself in the wide sea. So I unhappily, to find a mother and a brother, do lose myself."

_____ 3. "The capon burns, and the pig falls from the spit, and the meat will be all cold if you do not come home."

_____ 4. "Because I familiarly sometimes chat with you, you presume to jest with me in this free manner. I am not in a sportive humour now: where is the money?"

_____ 5. "Dowsabel claims me for a husband: but I must go, for servants must obey their masters, commands."

_____ 6. "The venomous clamor of a jealous woman is a more deadly poison than a mad dog's tooth."

_____ 7. "She has betrayed me to my own reproof."

## 4 Comprehension: Choose the correct answer.

_____ 1. What was the cause for the Syracusan merchant Aegeon to have ventured to come to the city of Ephesus, which was death for him?
   a) To find out what had become of his wife and eldest child.
   b) To beg or borrow money from its citizens to pay for a debt.
   c) To relate the events of his unfortunate life.
   d) To search for his youngest son and was unwilling to leave there unsought.

_____ 2. What did the fishermen do after they took up Aegeon's wife and the children?
   a) They took them away from her and sold them to the uncle of the duke of Ephesus.
   b) They saved Aegeon and the other two babies and landed them in safety at Syracuse.
   c) They came to Ephesus to observe the manners of the people.
   d) They made Aegeon's wife enter a nunnery.

_____ 3. What kind of a fellow is Drumio of Syracuse?
   a) He was a clumsy fellow and was known as a troublemaker.
   b) He had the old habit of pocketing his master's money.
   c) He used to divert his master with odd humors and merry jests.
   d) He was of a dull and melancholy disposition.

_____ 4. What was Dromio of Syracuse surprised at in Adriana's house?
   a) That his master was very much pleased with Luciana.
   b) That her cook-maid claimed him for her husband.
   c) That his brother had a wife.
   d) That his master could find pretence to get away.

_____ 5. What did the married Antipholus do when he was denied entrance into his own house?
   a) He ordered Dromio to get his things on board a ship, not choosing to stay there any longer.

b) He cried out to the duke for justice, telling him that his wife was driving him mad.

c) He went and dined with the lady whom his wife had often accused him of visiting.

d) He beat Dromio for not having knocked the door down.

____ 6. What did Antipholus of Syracuse call the lady who asked him for a gold chain?
a) A shrew.          b) A sorceress.
c) An abbess.        d) A prostitute.

____ 7. What did Adriana do when she was convinced that her husband was mad?
a) She ordered her servants to bind her husband with ropes, and conveyed him into a dark room.

b) She insisted that the abbess have her husband delivered up to a doctor.

c) She cried out to the duke for help to cure him of his madness.

d) She constantly reprehended him for loving any lady better than her.

____ 8. The following happened at sunset of Aegeon's day in Ephesus, except:
a) Antipholus of Ephesus denied all knowledge of him.

b) He found his son Antipholus of Syracuse.

c) The abbess made herself known to be his long-lost wife.

d) Antipholus of Syracuse married the fair Luciana.

---

## 5 Discussion

1. What harm did jealousy do to Adrian and Antipholus of Ephesus?

2. The errors in this comedy happened due to a series of coincidences. What do you think of coincidences? What power do they have to influence people?

3. Do you agree that *The Comedy of Errors* is a play for pure entertainment? Do you think it involves any serious issues as some of Shakespeare's plays do?

## 6   Stage a Scene

Prepare a scene you and your partners enjoy the most. Try to solve the problems in your small production.

1. Who are you going to cast as the two pairs of twins if there are no real twins in your team?
2. What kind of acting exercises or preparations do you need to make them identical?

## 7   Design a Poster

Design a poster for a real production of The Comedy of Errors. You could use sketches, paintings, photographs from the rehearsing scenes, or computer processed pictures as the main image. On the poster, be sure to put some basic information:

1. the production crew;
2. cast;
3. dates, times and locations of performance;
4. ticket prices;
5. where or how to get the tickets; and
6. sponsors (if any).

## 《連環錯》 **Answers**

### 2 Vocabulary
**A.**

1. ransom
2. importuned
3. custody
4. solitary
5. infancy
6. persisting
7. bewitched
8. illusions
9. freaks
10. lunatic

### 3 Identification
**B.**

1. Aegeon
2. Antipholus of Syracuse
3. Dromio of Ephesus
4. Antipholus of Syracuse
5. Dromio of Syracuse
6. the abbess
7. Adriana
8. Duke of Ephesus

### 4 Comprehension

1. d
2. a
3. c
4. b
5. c
6. b
7. a
8. d

**P.26** 威尼斯有一位叫做賽拉客的猶太人，他是個放高利貸的人，靠著借錢給基督徒商人收取高利息，積攢了很多財富。

賽拉客為人刻薄，借出去的錢錙銖必討，所以善良人家都瞧不起他，有一個叫做安東尼的年輕威尼斯商人尤其討厭他。賽拉客也很痛恨安東尼，因為安東尼常借錢給落難的人，而且不取分毫利息，這位貪婪的猶太人和這位慷慨的商人安東尼，因此結下了樑子。安東尼只要在市場或交易所撞見賽拉客，就會斥責他放高利貸，是個不厚道的生意人。這個猶太人會在表面上做出耐心聽教的樣子，但心裡時常琢磨著要報復。

**P.28** 安東尼是個好心人，而且他家道殷實，待人謙恭有禮。在義大利，就屬他最能發揚古羅馬的光榮了，所以全城的市民都很喜愛他。他有個好朋友，一個叫做巴薩紐的威尼斯貴族。巴薩紐的祖產不多，卻有財薄的公孫王子的毛病，他揮金如土，不自量力，他那一點家產都快被他散盡。而他只要一缺錢用，安東尼就會接濟他，他們看起來簡直是共用同一顆心、同一個錢包。

這一天，巴薩紐來找安東尼，說他想和一位心儀的富家千金成親，也可以藉此改善自己的經濟狀況。這位千金剛剛喪父，是大筆遺產的唯一繼承人。她父親在世時，巴薩紐常去她家串門子，巴薩紐覺得她對自己有意思，似乎有意要他來提親。然而，他沒有資金打理自己的門面來匹配這位富有的繼承人。所以來求安東尼好人做到底，再借給他三千元。

**P.29** 安東尼當時手頭上並沒有錢，不過他想自己有批載貨的船隻很快就會進港，便表示要去找有錢的放債人賽拉客，以押船隻的方式來向他借錢。

安東尼和巴薩紐便一道去找賽拉客。安東尼請猶太人借他三千元，利息隨他開，他會用海上那些船隻所裝載的貨物來還債。

**P.30** 賽拉客聽了心下琢磨道：「要是讓我抓到他的把柄，我就要痛痛快快地把前仇舊恨一次算清楚。他恨我們猶太民族，借錢給別人又不收利息，還在別人面前數落我，罵我正當掙來的錢是高利貸。我要是此仇不報，就詛咒我們猶太人吧！」

見他沉思不語，急著用錢的安東尼說：「賽拉客，你聽見了沒？錢到底借不借？」

**P.31** 猶太人聽了答道：「安東尼先生，您三番兩次在市場裡斥喝我借

15

錢放高利貸，我都只是聳聳肩，吞忍了下來，因為受苦是我們的民族性。你又說我是異教徒，是殺人狗，你往我的猶太長袍吐口水，還用腳踢我，把我當成流浪狗一樣。那好了，你現在需要我的幫忙，就跑來找我說：『賽拉客，借錢給我。』狗會有錢嗎？流浪狗借得出三千元嗎？我是不是應該卑躬屈膝地說，好先生，您上星期三吐我口水，又有一次您說我是狗，念及這些情份，我應該借錢給您。」

安東尼回答：「我還是有可能再那樣叫你，或是再吐你口水、再踢你幾腳。你借我錢，犯不著當是借錢給朋友，寧可當是借錢給敵人。要是我沒錢還，你大可扳起臉來，按條約行事。」

「怎麼，看看你！氣成這樣！我願意和你做兄弟，得到你的厚愛。我會忘掉你對我的侮辱，你要借多少就借多少，我半分利息也不要。」賽拉客說。

**P.32** 聽到這個好心的提議，安東尼很驚訝。一副假慈悲的賽拉客說，他這麼做只是想得到安東尼的友誼，並再度強調他願意借他三千元，而且不收利息，只要他願意和他去律師那裡簽下借據玩玩：如期未還，當割身上一磅肉，所割之處，隨賽拉客之意。

安東尼回答：「好，我就簽了借條，而且我還會說猶太人的心腸真是好啊。」

**P.33** 巴薩紐認為安東尼不該為他簽下這種借據，但安東尼執意要簽，他想借約到期之前，他的船隻就會帶著數倍於此價的貨物回來。

賽拉客聽到他們在討論，便喊道：「啊！我父亞伯拉罕，這些基督徒的疑心病真重！他們自己交易不仁，就懷疑別人的動機。巴薩紐，請你告訴我，要是他未能如期付款，我逼我要那份賠償有什麼用？一磅人肉，從人身上削下來的肉，比羊肉、牛肉都還不值錢，有什麼油水可撈呀。我是為了討好他才賣這份人情，如果他要，那就成交，不然我就送客了。」

猶太人口口聲聲說他是出於好意，但巴薩紐仍不願好友為了他冒這種可怕賠償的險。但安東尼還是不肯聽勸，覺得那不過是鬧著玩的（如那猶太人所說），便簽下了借據。

**P.34** 巴薩紐想娶的富有繼承人住在一個叫做背芒特的地方，離威尼斯不遠。她的名字叫做波兒榭，無論是人品或才智，她一點都不輸給我們在書上讀過的那位波兒榭——加圖之女，布魯托之妻。

在好友安東尼冒生命危險給予慷慨的資助後，巴薩紐帶著一行衣著光鮮的隨從，由一名叫做葛提諾的紳士陪同，前往背芒特。

巴薩紐的求婚過程很順利，波兒榭很快便答應了這門親事。

巴薩紐向波兒榭坦誠自己沒有家產，能夠誇耀的只有自己系出名門，具有貴族血統。波兒榭愛的是巴薩紐的人品，況且她自己家財萬貫，並不在乎夫婿的家業。她優雅恭謙地答道，但願自己能再美個千倍、再富個萬倍，這樣才好匹配他。甚有教養的波兒榭還合宜地謙稱，說自己無學無術，涉世未深，但幸而年紀還輕，尚能學習，凡事都願意虛心受教、蒙他教誨。她表示：

**P.36** 「我的人和我的東西現在都歸你了。巴薩紐，我昨天還是這棟豪宅的主人，是自己的女王，是僕人的主人。如今這棟房子、這些僕人和我自己，都歸你了。我就用這枚戒指做為憑藉，獻上一切。」說罷便遞給巴薩紐一枚戒指。

　　富裕高貴的波兒榭親切地接受了一個家產微薄的丈夫，巴薩紐一方面很感激，一方面也很驚喜。這位親愛的女子如此敬待他，他不知該如何表達喜悅和敬意，只是斷斷續續說了些愛慕和感謝的話。他接過戒指，發誓會永遠戴著戒指，不會拔下來。

　　葛提諾和波兒榭的貼身侍女涅芮莎，各自在旁侍奉自己的主人和小姐。看到波兒榭這樣得體地答應做巴薩紐的賢妻，葛提諾便向巴薩紐和慷慨的小姐道喜，並要求准允他也能在同時間結婚。

　　「葛提諾，我打從心底贊成，只要你能找到個妻子。」巴薩紐說。

**P.38** 葛提諾這才說他心上中意波兒榭小姐的美麗侍女涅芮莎，而涅芮莎也允諾過他，只要小姐和巴薩紐成親，她就嫁給他。波兒榭問涅芮莎是否真有此事。

　　涅芮莎回道：「夫人，的確如此，如您同意的話。」

　　波兒榭樂而允之。巴薩紐高興地說道：「葛提諾，你們這樣一成親，我們的婚禮就更添光彩了。」

**P.39** 這時，這兩對情人歡天喜地的氣氛，卻被一位走進門來的信差給打斷了。他捎來一封安東尼寫來的信，上面寫著駭人的消息。

　　巴薩紐看著安東尼的信，臉色慘白。波兒榭擔心那封信是通知巴薩紐好友的死訊，便問是什麼消息讓他這麼難過。他回答：「啊，親愛的波兒榭，這張紙上寫著些最悲慘的消息。好夫人，我當初向妳表白情意時，向妳坦承妳僅有的財富就是我的貴族血統，但我當時應該也要告訴妳，我不僅一文不值，而且還債台高築。」

　　巴薩紐把我們前面提過的事告訴波兒榭：他向安東尼借錢，安東尼為此跑去跟猶太人賽拉客調錢，簽下借條──若如期不還，就用一磅肉來償債。巴薩紐讀安東尼的信，信上寫著：

P.40 摯友巴薩紐，我的船隻出事了，借據被猶太人扣住。

償債之後，我性命必不保，臨死之前，再盼見你一面。

但得依你興致，若情份不足以邀你前來，便莫為此信而來。

「哦，相公！你盡快把事情安排之後就趕過去吧，你可以用多於二十倍的錢去還債。絕不可以因為我的巴薩紐的過失，而讓這位仁慈的好友傷到一根毫髮。既然你是我用這麼高的代價所贖來的，我會格外珍惜你的。」波兒榭說。

波兒榭表示兩人要在巴薩紐動身之前成親，好讓他有權合法使用她的財產。於是當天他們倆就和葛提諾與涅芮莎雙雙完成婚事。婚禮一結束，巴薩紐和葛提諾便急忙趕往威尼斯。當巴薩紐見到安東尼時，安東尼已經鋃鐺入獄了。

P.42 還債期限已過，狠心的猶太人不肯收巴薩紐還給他的錢，堅持要安東尼的一磅肉。威尼斯公爵審判這宗驚人案例的日子已經敲定，巴薩紐憂心如焚地等待判決結果。

P.43 丈夫離行前，波兒榭振奮地和他說話，並囑咐他回來時也要把他那位摯友一道帶回來。然而，她心裡仍擔心安東尼難逃一劫，她獨自思量著是否可以幫上忙，救出相公巴薩紐的好友。她願意尊重她的巴薩紐，就像她曾用為人妻子的婉約態度表示，他比她聰明，她凡事都願聽從丈夫的指示。然而，現在眼見她所敬重的丈夫的好友面臨危險，她就不得不採取行動了。她毫不懷疑自己的本事，單憑她準確完美的判斷力，她當下便決定親自到威尼斯去為安東尼辯護。

波兒榭有個親戚是辯護律師，叫做貝拉里。她寫信跟他說明這件案情，尋求他的意見，並請他回信時寄上一套辯護律師的服裝。

P.44 派去的信差返回時，帶回了貝拉里說明要如何進行辯護的建議，以及所須的裝備。

波兒榭和侍女涅芮莎換上男裝。她套上律師袍，帶著扮成書記的涅芮莎隨行。兩人立即動身出發，在審判日當天趕到了威尼斯。

P.45 波兒榭走進元老院這個高等法庭時，案子正當著公爵和威尼斯元老面前即將開審。她遞上貝拉里的信，這個博學的辯護律師在寫給公爵的信裡表示，他原本要親自為安東尼辯護，但因病無法出庭，故請求允許博學的年輕博士包薩澤（他是這麼稱呼波兒榭的）代他辯護。

公爵一方面批准請求，一面打量著這陌生人的年輕相貌：她披著律師袍，頭上戴著一頂大大的假髮，偽裝得沒有半點破綻。

重大的審判開始。波兒榭環顧四下，看到狠心的猶太人和巴薩紐，不過巴薩紐沒有認出來喬裝的波兒榭。巴薩紐就站在安東尼的旁邊，他為朋友提心吊膽，焦慮不安。

**P.47** 想到這項艱鉅任務事關重大，波兒榭這婉約女子激出了勇氣。她毫不怯場地執行自己擔當的職責，她先對賽拉客發言，說明根據威尼斯的法律，他有權索取借據寫明的賠償。接著她大大說了一番仁慈的美德，任誰聽了都會動容，除了冷血的賽拉客。她說，仁慈就像從天降到塵世的甘露，是雙倍的福分，保佑施者，也保佑受者。對君王而言，仁慈更勝於王冠，因為仁慈本身就是上帝的一種屬性。執法時越能夠秉持仁慈，這份世俗的權力就越接近上帝。她要賽拉客記得我們都祈求上天仁慈，而同樣的禱文也應教會我們對待別人也要仁慈。

賽拉客只回答她說，他要索取借據上寫明的賠償。

「他沒有能力還錢嗎？」波兒榭問。

**P.48** 巴薩紐表示，隨便猶太人要多於三千元幾倍的錢都可以。但賽拉客不肯，仍堅持要安東尼的一磅肉。巴薩紐乞求博學的年輕辯護律師想辦法稍微變通一下法律，救救安東尼的性命。但波兒榭嚴正地回答，律法一旦訂立，就絕不容更改。

聽到波兒榭說法律不得擅改，賽拉客覺得她反倒在為自己辯護，便說道：「但以理再世來審判了！啊，明智的年輕律師！我深深敬仰您！您要比您的外表資深多了！」

波兒榭要賽拉客讓她瞧瞧借據。她看完借據，說道：「就依這張借據做出賠償，這位猶太人依約可以合法索取安東尼心窩處削下的一磅肉。」然後她對賽拉客說：「你還是發發慈悲，把錢收下，讓我把這紙借條撕掉吧。」

狠心的賽拉客不肯寬容，他說：「我用我的靈魂發誓，再如何能言善道的人，也不能說動我。」

**P.49** 波兒榭說：「既然如此，安東尼，你的心臟就準備挨刀子吧！」賽拉客興沖沖磨著長刀準備剮肉時，波兒榭對安東尼說：「你有話要說嗎？」

安東尼鎮定豁然地答道，他已經準備就死，無話可說。接著他對巴薩紐說：「巴薩紐，把手給我！再會了！不要因為我為你所遭遇的劫數而難過。在尊夫人面前為我說好話，告訴她我有多愛你！」

**P.50** 巴薩紐非常沉痛，他答道：「安東尼，我娶了個妻子，我視她如自己的性命一般的珍貴，但我這條命、我的妻子和這整個世界，都還不及你的性命珍貴！為了救你，我寧願失去一切，把所有一切都給這個惡徒。」

聽到丈夫言語激動地說出對摯友安東尼的愛，善良的姑娘波兒榭雖不以為忤，但仍不禁表示：「要是尊夫人在場，聽了你這番話，諒她不見得會感激你吧！」

老愛仿傚主人的葛提諾心想，他總也得學學巴薩紐說段話。此時做書記員打扮的涅芮莎正在波兒榭的一旁做記錄，葛提諾便對她說道：「我有個妻子，我也發誓我愛她，但我希望她就在天堂裡，好請求上帝改變這個狗猶太人的殘忍個性。」

「還好你是背著她說出了這個願望，不然你家裡恐怕要雞犬不寧了。」涅芮莎說。

賽拉客這會兒不耐煩地嚷著：「我們是在浪費時間，我請求宣布判決。」

P.52 法庭一時之間瀰漫可怕的預感，每顆心都為安東尼傷痛不已。

波兒榭先問秤肉的磅秤是否備妥，然後對猶太人說：「賽拉客，你得找位外科醫生在旁看顧，以免他流血太多致死。」

賽拉客的本意就是讓安東尼失血過多而死，便說道：「借據上並未明載。」

波兒榭回答：「借據上未寫明又有什麼關係？你做點善事總是好的。」

對此賽拉客只是回答：「我看不到借據上有這一條。」

波兒榭說：「那麼你可以取安東尼的一磅肉了，法律許可，法庭也批准。你可以割下他胸口上的肉，法律許可，法庭也批准。」

賽拉客又喊道：「啊！明智正直的法官！但以理下世審判了！」他磨著長刀，虎視眈眈望著安東尼，說道：「來吧，準備好了！」

P.54 「等等，猶太人！還有件一事，這借條上沒有允諾給你血，條文寫的是『一磅肉』。所以你削那磅肉時，只要讓這位基督徒流下半滴血，那你的土地和財產就都要依法沒收充公，歸給威尼斯政府。」波兒榭說。

要賽拉客把肉割下而不讓安東尼流血，根本就是天方夜譚嘛。借條上明載的是肉而不是血，波兒榭就憑這一個巧思，救了安東尼一命。元老院裡響遍了喝采聲，眾人無不讚嘆這位年輕律師的絕妙機智，想出了這麼妙的權宜之計。葛提諾鸚鵡學舌地學賽拉客喊道：「啊！明智正直的法官！猶太人，你看看，但以理下世審判了！」

P.55 看到自己的毒計無法得逞，賽拉客神情失望地表示願意收下錢。安東尼意外獲救，喜出望外的巴薩紐喊道：「錢在這裡！」

但波兒榭阻止了他，說道：「且慢，不用急。猶太人只能索取所

20

要求的賠償，所以，賽拉客，準備好割那塊肉吧。但是注意不要讓血流出來，而且也不可以少割或多割，只能剛剛好割下一磅。要是少割了或多割了一點點，磅秤顯示的重量有絲毫差距，那就得依威尼斯法律判你極刑，並由元老院沒收你的全部財產。」

「給我錢，我走！」賽拉客說。

「我已經準備好了！在這裡。」巴薩紐說。

賽拉客正要伸手拿錢時，波兒榭再度阻止了他，說道：「等等，猶太人，你還有個把柄在我手上。依威尼斯法律，你因為意圖謀害一位威尼斯市民的性命，所以你的財產要充公歸給政府，而你的性命就看公爵是否願意開恩了。你就跪下吧，請求他饒恕你。」

P.56 公爵於是對賽拉客說：「讓你瞧瞧我們基督徒的精神有什麼不一樣，不用等你開口，我就饒你一命。你的財富半數歸安東尼，半數歸公給政府。」

寬宏大量的安東尼接著說，只要賽拉客肯寫下契據，死後將財產留給女兒和女婿，他就願意放棄賽拉客的那一份財產。安東尼知道猶太人有個獨生女，最近不顧他的反對嫁給一個基督徒，對方是安東尼的朋友，叫做勞倫佐。賽拉客為此震怒不已，於是取消了她的財產繼承權。

P.57 猶太人答應了這個條件。他復仇不成，財產又被剝奪，便說道：「我人不舒服，讓我回去吧。隨後再把契據送來給我，我會簽字，把我的一半財產留給我女兒。」

「那你就回去，但你得先簽字。你要是後悔自己為人殘酷，並改信基督，那政府可寬免你另一半財產的罰鍰。」公爵說。

公爵釋放安東尼，宣布退庭。之後，他對年輕律師的足智多謀讚不絕口，並邀他到家裡吃飯。

為了比丈夫提前一步回到背芒特，波兒榭答道：「承蒙厚愛，感激不盡，不過我得馬上趕回去。」

公爵表示，很可惜他沒空留下來一道吃飯。他轉向安東尼，補了一句說：「好好酬謝這位先生吧，我想這次多虧了他。」

P.58 公爵和眾元老離開法庭後，巴薩紐對波兒榭說：「最令人敬重的先生呀，多虧了您的機智，我和我的朋友安東尼今天才得以免掉可怕的刑罰。這原本要還給猶太人的三千元，就請您收下吧。」

安東尼說：「您的大恩大德，我們將終身報答。」

波兒榭說什麼也不肯接受那筆錢，但巴薩紐仍堅持她應該接受一些報償。她說：「那就把你的手套送給我吧，讓我戴著它做紀念。」

待巴薩紐脫下手套後，她瞥見他手指上那枚她送的戒指。原來這位機靈的姑娘是想弄到他的戒指，等之後見到巴薩紐時，可以拿這個來跟他開開玩笑，所以才向他要手套。瞥見這枚戒指後，她說：「承蒙厚愛，那我就拿你這個戒指吧。」

P.59 巴薩紐很苦惱，律師想要的是他唯一不能離手的東西。他很為難地表示，戒指是妻子所贈，他發過誓要終身戴著，故不便奉送。但他願意張掛榜文，找出威尼斯最珍貴的戒指來送給他。

波兒榭一聽，便佯裝受到屈辱。她走出法庭，說道：「先生，你倒是教了我該如何應付乞丐。」

安東尼說：「親愛的巴薩紐，你就把戒指給他吧。看在我的情誼和他幫了這個大忙的份上，就得罪嫂子一次吧。」

看到自己這種忘恩負義的樣子，巴薩紐感到慚愧，就讓步了。他派葛提諾帶著戒指去追波兒榭。結果，同樣給過葛提諾戒指的書記涅芮莎，也向他要戒指，葛提諾便一起奉送出去（他絕不讓主人的慷慨專美於前）。

兩位姑娘想著，等她們回到家，可以如何地指責丈夫將戒指送出去，並一口咬定是送給哪個女人了。她們想到這裡，不禁笑了出來。

P.60 回家路上，波兒榭想著自己做了一件善事，心裡很快樂。她心情愉快，所見的一切都分外美好：今晚的月光前所未有的皎潔，後來賞心悅目的月亮躲進了雲堆裡，這時從背芒特家中所透出的一道光線，讓她的想像更加歡樂地奔馳著。她對涅芮莎說：「我們看到的那道光線是從家中廳堂照出來的，一根小小的蠟燭，竟能照耀得這麼遠。同樣地，在濁世裡，一件善事也夠發出光芒。」聽到從家裡傳來音樂聲，她說：「這音樂聽起來，我覺得比白天的聲音要悅耳多了。」

波兒榭和涅芮莎進到家門，換上自己的衣服，等丈夫回來。不一會兒，丈夫們就帶著安東尼回到家。巴薩紐把他的摯友介紹給波兒榭夫人，她的祝賀歡迎之言尚未說完，他們就看到涅芮莎和丈夫在角落裡吵架。

「怎麼一下子就拌起嘴來了呢？怎麼回事？」波兒榭問。

P.61 葛提諾回答：「夫人，就為了涅芮莎給我的那個廉價鍍金戒指，上面還刻著刀匠刻在刀子上的那種詩句：愛我，勿棄我。」

「詩或戒指代表什麼意義？我給你戒指時，你對我發誓會戴到生命的最後一刻，而你現在卻說你送給律師的書記了。我知道你一定是把它送給別的女人了。」涅芮莎說。

「我舉手發誓，我送給一個年輕人，一個男孩，他個頭小小的，

22

不比妳高。他是那個年輕辯護律師的書記，多虧那位律師的機智辯護，才救了安東尼一命。那個聒噪男孩就跟我要戒指以作為報酬，我說什麼也不能拒絕他啊。」葛提諾回答。

P.62 波兒樹說：「葛提諾，這就是你的不對了，竟然捨棄妻子所贈送的第一份禮物。我也送給我丈夫巴薩紐一枚戒指，我敢說他無論如何也不會捨棄那枚戒指。」

為了掩飾自己的過失，葛提諾回道：「就是因為主人巴薩紐把他的戒指送給了那個辯護律師，所以那個辛苦抄寫的書記男孩才會跟我要戒指的。」

一聽到這裡，波兒樹佯裝發怒，責怪巴薩紐把她的戒指送給別人。她說她相信涅芮莎的話，戒指一定是送給了哪個女人。

惹火了自己心愛的夫人，巴薩紐很難過，他懇切地說道：「不，我以人格擔保，戒指不是給別的女人，而是給了一位法學博士。他不肯接受我送的三千元，卻要我的戒指。我不答應他，他就快快不樂地走了。親愛的波兒樹，我能怎麼辦呢？看到自己如此忘恩負義，我很慚愧，只得教人追上去，把戒指送給他。好夫人，原諒我啊。妳當時要是也在場，我想妳會要求我把戒指送給那位可敬的博士。」

「哎！你們會吵架，都是因為我的緣故。」安東尼說。

P.64 波兒樹請安東尼不要自責，不管如何，他們都很歡迎他。安東尼表示：「為了巴薩紐，我曾經押了自己的身體。多虧那個妳丈夫送上戒指的人，不然我早就魂歸西天了。我敢再立一張契據，用我的靈魂做抵押，擔保妳丈夫絕不會再對妳背信了。」

「那你就當他的保證人吧。把這枚戒指拿給他，叫他可得更加小心地妥善保存。」波兒樹說。

巴薩紐一看，發現這個戒指和他送出去的一模一樣，不禁吃了一驚。這時波兒樹才告訴他，她就是那個年輕的辯護律師，而涅芮莎就是她的書記。巴薩紐心裡說不出的又驚又喜，原來正是因為妻子卓越的勇氣和智慧，才救了安東尼一命。

波兒樹再一次對安東尼表示歡迎，還把無意中落到她手裡的信交給他。信上寫著，安東尼那批原本以為出事的船隻，都已經安全進港。

P.65 就這樣，這位富商故事的悲慘開端，因為出乎意料的好運而讓人遺忘了。他們有的是閒情來笑談戒指的事情，還有兩位不識妻子的丈夫。葛提諾用押韻的話，開心地起誓：

人生在世，唯怕一事，持涅芮莎的戒指，誠惶誠恐。

# 《連環錯》中譯

**P.81** 溪洛窟和以弗所兩國不合。以弗所制定一條屬法，明文規定溪洛窟的商人只要在以弗所市被發現，就得繳贖金一千馬克，否則一律處斬。

有人在以弗所街上發現溪洛窟的老商人葉吉，他被押去見公爵，看是要繳大筆罰金，還是接受死刑。

葉吉沒有錢付罰金，公爵在宣判他的死刑之前，要他說明自己的身世，以及為何明知溪洛窟商人進以弗所市會被處死，仍冒死前來。

葉吉說他不怕死，因為他早就痛不欲生了。要他講他那不幸的一生，才是最痛苦的事。以下，他開始說出自己的故事：

**P.82** 「我在溪洛窟出生，從小就學做買賣。娶了妻子後，生活過得還算幸福。有一次，我要去掀披丹一趟，因為做生意的關係，我在那裡待了半年。後來知道自己還得停留更久，就請妻子也一道過來。她人一到，就生下兩個兒子。很奇怪，兩個兒子長得一模一樣，根本沒辦法分辨誰是誰。

我妻子生這對孿生兄弟時，在她下榻的客棧裡有另一個窮人家的婦女也生了兩個兒子。這對雙胞胎也和我兩個兒子一樣，彼此長得非常相像。因為他們的父母親太窮，所以我就買下他們，想說養大後可以侍奉我的兩個兒子。

**P.83** 我的兒子長得很英俊，妻子深感驕傲。她日夜想著回家，我只得答應。我們在不祥的時刻上了船，因為我們從掀披丹出航還不到一浬時，就刮起可怕的暴風雨。風雨愈來愈大，船員們眼看大船不保，為了逃命，他們就擠上小艇，把我們丟在船上，我們隨時都可能被狂風大浪給淹沒。

**P.84** 我妻子一直哭，那些不知道害怕的可愛孩子看到媽媽在哭，也跟著哭了起來。我自己並不怕死，但看到他們哭，我為他們感到惶恐，一心只想著如何可以保護他們的安全。我學航海人那套對抗暴風雨的方法，把小兒子綁在一根備用小船桅的一端，另一端則綁著孿生奴僕的弟弟。我教妻子如法炮製，把另外兩個孩子也綁在另一根船桅上。

她看著兩個哥哥，我看著兩個弟弟。我們又各自把自己綁在綁著孩子的船桅上，要不是靠著這個方法，我們早就死了，因為船撞上了大礁石，都撞碎了。我們抓著細長的船桅，在水面上漂浮。我要照顧兩個孩子，無法顧及我的妻子，不久她就和其他兩個孩子與我分散了。

他們還在我的視線範圍內時，被一艘（我認為是）哥林斯來的漁艇救了起來。

P.86 看到他們獲救後，為了我的寶貝兒子和小奴僕，我拼命地和怒濤狂浪搏鬥。最後我們也被一艘船救了起來。那些水手認得我，很親切地招呼並幫助我們，把我們安全地送到溪洛窟的岸上。但從那個不幸的一刻起，我就再也沒有妻子和大兒子的下落了。

現在，我唯一在意的人就是我的么兒。他十八歲時開始打聽母親和哥哥的下落，時常央求我讓他帶著奴僕出去找他們。他的那個奴僕，就是那個也和哥哥失散了的小奴僕。最後我勉強答應了他，我是很渴望得到妻子和長子的消息，可是讓我的么兒去找他們，我也可能失去他和小奴僕啊。

P.87 如今，我兒子離開我已經有七年了。這五年來，我走遍世界，到處尋找他們。我到過希臘最遠的邊境，穿越亞洲，沿著海岸回來，在以弗所登陸，只要是有人跡的地方，我都不放過。但我這一生就要在今天落幕了，只要能夠確知我的妻子和兩個兒子都還活著，那我死也瞑目了。」

不幸的葉吉說完了他的悲慘遭遇後，公爵很同情這個不幸的父親，他因為疼愛失散的兒子才落難。公爵說，他的職權地位不允許他擅改法律，要不是因為有違法令，他大可把他給放了。最後，公爵並沒有嚴依律文將他立刻處斬，而是給他一天的時間去籌錢來付罰金。

P.88 對葉吉來說，這一天的寬限又有何用？他在以弗所人生地不熟，要找人借他一千馬克來付罰金，談何容易。沒有人可以搭救，何從釋放？他在獄卒的押解下，從公爵那裡退了庭。

葉吉以為他在以弗所沒有半個熟識，可是就在他遍尋么兒而性命堪虞時，他的么兒和長子卻恰巧都在以弗所城內。

P.89 葉吉的兩個兒子不僅容貌和身材完全一樣，連名字也都叫做安提弗，而另外那一對孿生奴僕，也都取名拙米歐。葉吉的么兒是來自溪洛窟的安提弗，老人家來以弗所，就是為了找他。好巧不巧的是，安提弗帶著奴僕拙米歐，和父親在同一天來到了以弗所。他也是溪洛窟商人，和父親的處境一樣危險。但幸虧他遇見了一個友人，通知他有個溪洛窟老商人落難的事情，勸他冒充成披丹商人，他接受了友人的建議。聽到自己的同胞處境危急，他很難過，只是萬萬沒想到，這個老商人就是自己的父親。

P.90 葉吉的長子住在以弗所已經有二十年了（姑且稱他是「大安提弗」，以便和弟弟「小安提弗」做區別），而且還是個富人，有能力支付罰金，贖回父親的性命。只不過大安提弗對父親一無所知，他和母親被漁夫從海上救起來時，年紀還很小，只記得被救時的樣子，對父母親都沒有印象了。把大安提弗、母親和小奴僕拙米歐救起來的漁夫，從母親身邊帶走了兩個小孩（這位不幸的婦人傷心極了），打算賣掉他們。

　　漁夫把大安提弗和大拙米歐賣給了知名的軍人梅納封公爵。他是以弗所公爵的叔父，他去以弗所探訪他的公爵姪兒時，隨身也帶了這兩個孩子。

**P.91** 以弗所公爵很喜歡大安提弗，等大安提弗長大後，就讓他在自己的軍隊裡擔任軍官。大安提弗驍勇善戰，在沙場上建功，還救了提拔他的公爵一命。於是公爵就把以弗所一位富家姑娘雅卓安娜賜婚給他。在父親來到以弗所時，大安提弗已和雅卓安娜住在一起（他的奴僕大拙米歐也侍候著他）。

　　小安提弗和那個建議他冒充成掖披丹人的友人分開後，就遞給奴僕小拙米歐一些錢，要他先帶著錢到準備去用餐的客棧，表示自己要去鎮上蹓躂蹓躂，看看當地的風土民情。

**P.93** 小拙米歐是個很得人緣的傢伙。小安提弗發悶發愁時，他會用奴僕那種古怪幽默和逗趣的俏皮話來自娛娛人。也因此，比起一般的主僕關係，小拙米歐對小安提弗講話的樣子就顯得比較隨便。

　　小安提弗打發小拙米歐走了後，兀自站了半晌，尋思自己孤身一人到處尋找母親和哥哥，至今每個地方都打聽不出半點下落。他悲傷地自言自語：「我就像海洋中的一滴水，出去尋找自己的水滴同伴，結果在茫茫大海之中迷失了自己。我如此不幸，想找母親和哥哥，結果卻連自己也迷失了。」

**P.94** 就在他想著令人疲憊又毫無結果的尋人之旅時，（他以為）小拙米歐回來了。他納悶他怎麼這麼快就回來，便問他把錢擱在哪裡了。然而，現在和他說話的這個人並不是他自己的小拙米歐，而是孿生哥哥大拙米歐，和大安提弗住在一塊。

　　這一對拙米歐和這一對安提弗，雙雙還是長得一模一樣，一如葉吉在他們嬰兒時期所見的一樣。因此也難怪安提弗會以為是自己的奴僕回來了，還問他怎麼這麼快就回來了。

　　大拙米歐回答：「夫人要我請您回去吃飯。您再不回去的話，雞肉就要烤焦，肉串上的豬肉就要掉下來冷掉了。」

　　「現在不是開玩笑的時候。你把錢放在哪裡了？」小安提弗說。但大拙米歐仍自顧說著夫人要他來請安提弗回去吃飯，小安提弗問道：

「什麼夫人？」

P.95 「老爺，當然是您的夫人了。」大拙米歐答道。

這個小安提弗還是個光棍，他對大拙米歐發脾氣說：「我平時跟你隨便閒扯慣了，結果就讓你這樣放肆地開我玩笑。我現在沒有心情開玩笑，錢呢？我們在這裡人生地不熟的，這麼一大筆錢你不好好保管，怎麼敢放心？」

大拙米歐聽到主人（他以為那是他的主人）說他們人生地不熟，以為是小安提弗在開玩笑，就開心地回答：「老爺，請您坐下來吃飯時再開玩笑吧。我只負責把您請回家，和夫人及夫人的妹妹一起吃飯。」

這下小安提弗再也忍不住，他揍了大拙米歐一頓。大拙米歐跑回家，告訴夫人說，老爺不肯回來吃飯，還說他根本沒有老婆。

P.96 聽到老公說他沒有老婆，大安提弗的太太雅卓安娜大為光火。她本來就是個醋罈子，老是說丈夫移情別戀。她開始鬧情緒，大罵丈夫，說著難聽的醋話。跟她住在一起的妹妹露希安娜，勸她不要無憑無據地瞎猜，但她聽不進去。

小安提弗回到客棧，看到小拙米歐仍帶著錢，安然無事地待在客棧裡。看到小拙米歐，他準備再罵他亂開玩笑時，雅卓安娜這時正好出現。她認定自己看到的人就是她丈夫，便開口大罵，說他看她的眼神有多怪異（這也難怪，他初次見到這位氣呼呼的婦人）。她說他結婚之前是多愛麼她，現在卻琵琶別抱。

「老公，是怎麼回事？你怎麼不再愛我了？」她說。

「這位夫人，您在問我嗎？」大吃一驚的小安提弗問道。

P.98 他跟她說，他不是她的丈夫，他來以弗所才待了兩個鐘頭，但她不理會，一定要他跟她回家不可。小安提弗脫身不了，只得跟她一道回他哥哥的家，和雅卓安娜、妹妹一塊兒吃飯。她們一個叫他是丈夫，一個叫他是姐夫，弄得他莫名其妙，只好當自己在睡覺時娶了她，或是自己正在睡夢中。跟著一道前來的小拙米歐也一樣吃驚，因為嫁給他哥哥的那個廚娘，直喚他作丈夫。

就在小安提弗和嫂子吃飯時，他的哥哥（真正的丈夫）和大拙米歐想回家吃飯，但是僕人不肯放他們進門，因為夫人下令不讓任何人進來。他們一直敲門，當他們表示自己是安提弗和拙米歐時，女僕們都笑了出來。她們說安提弗正在和夫人吃飯，拙米歐也正在廚房裡。他們都快把門敲爛了，還是進不了門。最後大安提弗氣呼呼地離開，聽到有個男人正在和他太太吃飯，他覺得太怪了。

P.100 小安提弗吃完飯後，那位夫人仍滿口稱他是丈夫，而且他還聽

27

到連小拙米歐也被廚娘認作是丈夫。他百思不解，等一找到藉口開溜，就馬上逃出屋子。雖然他對妹妹露希安娜很有好感，但他並不喜歡愛吃醋的雅卓安娜，小拙米歐也很不滿意廚房裡的那位嬌妻，主僕兩人都巴不得盡快擺脫他們的新太太。

小安提弗一離開屋子，就碰上了金匠。金匠和雅卓安娜一樣，把他誤當成大安提弗。金匠叫了他一聲，遞給他一條金鍊子。小安提弗表示那不是他的東西，不肯收下。金匠只管回答那是依他的吩咐所打造的，說完就兀自離開，把金鍊子塞在他手裡。他想，自己在這裡遇到這些古怪的事情，一定是中了什麼法術，於是吩咐小拙米歐將行李打包上船，再也不想多留。

**P.102** 金匠把鍊子交出去之後，隨即因為一筆債務而被逮捕。金匠被官差逮捕時，已婚的大安提弗剛好打從旁邊經過。金匠以為已經把鍊子交給他，因此就跟他討金鍊子的錢。他剛給他的那條金鍊子的價錢，和那筆讓他現在被補的債務差不多。

大安提弗說他沒有拿到鍊子，金匠堅稱自己幾分鐘前才交給他的。他們都認為自己沒有錯，兩人爭執了好一會兒。大安提弗不認為金匠給過他鍊子，但因為兩兄弟長得一模一樣，所以金匠咬定已經把鍊子交到他手裡。最後，官差因金匠欠債未還要把他押進牢裡，又因大安提弗不付金鍊子的價錢，金匠要求官差一併逮捕他。於是他們爭吵的結果，就是兩人雙雙被帶走押入牢裡。

**P.104** 在被押去牢裡的路上，大安提弗碰見了小拙米歐，他把弟弟的奴僕誤認為自己的奴僕，吩咐他去找妻子雅卓安娜，要她把那筆害他被捕的錢送過來。

主人才從剛剛吃飯的那個古怪房子裡倉皇逃了出來，小拙米歐不明白現在怎麼又要他回去。他本是來通知主人船要開了，可是他不敢答話。他看主人不像可以開玩笑的樣子，就兀自離開。他咕噥著自己又得去雅卓安娜的家，說道：「到了那裡，陶紗貝又會說我是她丈夫了，可我還是得去呀，僕人只得聽主人的吩咐。」

雅卓安娜把錢交給小拙米歐，就在他要返回時，他碰到了小安提弗。這個小安提弗仍為一路上碰到的怪事感到納悶。哥哥在以弗所很有名氣，所以當他走在街上時，幾乎人人都向他打招呼，看起來就好像是熟人舊識一樣。有人要還他錢，說是欠他的，有人邀請他到家裡坐坐，有人說承蒙他好意幫忙，要跟他道謝，這些人都誤認他當成是他的哥哥。還有一個裁縫師拿絲綢給他看，說是替他買下來的，一定得幫他量身，好做衣服。

28

**P.106** 小安提弗開始覺得自己闖進了巫覡之國。小拙米歐一點也沒有能讓主人解開困惑，還問官差本來要抓他去坐牢，他怎麼逃出來了，然後把雅卓安娜派他拿去付贖金的那袋錢交給他。

小拙米歐說的什麼逮捕坐牢的事，還有他從雅卓安娜那裡帶來的錢，完全把小安提弗給搞糊塗了。他說：「拙米歐這傢伙一定是精神錯亂了，我們在幻境中徘徊。」他感到混亂恐慌，大喊道：「求上帝把我們從這個鬼地方救出去吧！」

這時走來一個陌生人，這回是個婦女，也叫他安提弗。她說，他那天和她一起吃過飯，她跟他要一條金鍊子，他答應了要給她。

**P.107** 小安提弗再也按捺不住了，斥罵她是妖女，說他不曾答應過要送她鍊子，不曾和她吃過飯，甚至在這之前都不曾見過她這張臉。那位女子一口咬定兩人曾一起吃過飯，他也答應過要送她鍊子。小安提弗繼續否認，她於是又說，她已經給了他一枚昂貴的戒指了，如果他不給她金鍊子，她就要收回她的戒指。

聽到這裡，小安提弗氣瘋了，直罵她是妖女、魔女，說自己從來就不認識她，也不知道她的什麼戒指，說完就跑開。聽到他這番話，又看到他憤怒的表情，女子愣在那裡。他們明明一起吃過飯，她也明明給過他戒指，所以他才答應要回送她金鍊子，這是再明白不過的事了。事實上她和其他人一樣都搞錯了，誤把他當成他哥哥，做那些事的是已婚的大安提弗，而不是眼前這位小安提弗。

**P.108** 已婚的大安提弗被擋在自己的家門口後（屋裡的人以為他已經在裡面了），便忿忿地離開。他的妻子最愛撚酸吃醋，他猜她一定是又吃了什麼飛醋。他想起她老愛亂冤枉他去找別的女人，為了報復她把他關在門外，他決定去找那位女子吃頓飯。那女子對他很客氣，被妻子這樣一番欺負之後，他就答應把原本打算送給妻子的金鍊子轉送給她。那條金鍊子後來被金匠誤交給他弟弟了。

女子很高興能有一條漂亮的金鍊子，所以也就回送已婚的大安提弗一枚戒指。當他說他根本不認識她、氣呼呼地走開時，她想他一定是發瘋了（她把他弟弟誤當成他）。於是她當下決定去找雅卓安娜，說她丈夫瘋了。

**P.109** 就在她把這件事告訴雅卓安娜時，大安提弗由一名獄卒陪著回來（獄卒准他回家拿錢還債），而雅卓安娜派小拙米歐送去的那一袋錢，早已交給小安提弗了。

聽到丈夫責怪她把他關在門外，雅卓安娜相信女子說她丈夫發瘋的事情一定錯不了。她又想起那整頓飯下來，丈夫一直否認是她的丈夫，還說生平今天第一次來以弗所。她想他一定是瘋了，因此付錢打發獄卒走了之後，就吩咐僕人用繩索把丈夫綁起來，帶到暗室裡，差人去請大夫來醫他的失心瘋。大安提弗一直激動地喊冤叫屈，要怪只怪他們兄弟長得一模一樣。他愈是生氣，大家就愈是確信他發瘋。至於大拙米歐，他也和主人說同樣的話，所以也就一起被綁起來帶走。

**P.111** 雅卓安娜把丈夫關起來後不久，一名僕人跑來告訴她，安提弗和拙米歐一定是從守衛那裡逃脫了，因為他們現在正逍遙自在地在旁邊的大街上走著。

雅卓安娜馬上帶了幾個人跑出去，要帶丈夫回來，而她妹妹也跟著一道出去。

他們來到附近一家修道院的門口時，碰見了小安提弗和小拙米歐。因為這兩對雙胞胎長得實在太相像，她們又再度認錯人。

因長相酷似，造成這一片混亂，小安提弗為此納悶不已。金匠給他的鍊子就掛在他脖子上，金匠卻責怪他不該否認拿了鍊子而不肯付錢。小安提弗反駁，鍊子是今天上午金匠送給他的，而且他早上過後就沒再見過金匠了。

**P.112** 這時雅卓安娜走到他旁邊，說他是她發了瘋的丈夫，從守衛那裡逃了出來。她隨行帶來的人準備動手強抓小安提弗和小拙米歐時，他們溜進修道院，安提弗央求院長讓他們躲在修道院裡。

女修道院院長親自出來詢問吵鬧的緣由。她是個認真可敬的女士，有智慧判斷所看到的事情。她不想魯莽交出到修道院尋求庇護的男子，便細問夫人她丈夫發瘋的事情。她問：「妳丈夫為什麼突然發瘋？他是損失了海上的財產，還是死了個知己好友，讓他精神錯亂？」

雅卓安娜回答不是這些原因。

修道院院長說：「還是說他愛上了某家小姐，不再那麼愛妳，所以變成了這個樣子？」

**P.114** 雅卓安娜表示，她早就懷疑他有外遇，所以才會常常不回家。

事實上，他並非另有他歡，而是妻子喜歡撩酸吃醋的個性逼得他有家難回（雅卓安娜激動的態度，讓院長猜出了是這個原因）。為了得知真相，院長說：「那妳真得好好罵罵他才對。」

「有啊，我罵他了啊。」雅卓安娜回答。

院長表示：「唉，那可能是罵得不夠兇。」

雅卓安娜很樂意讓院長相信她已經充分和安提弗談過這件事情了。她說：「我們整天都在談這事，床上談到這件事時，我就不讓他睡覺，餐桌上談到這件事時，我也不讓他吃飯。我們兩個單獨在一

30

起時，我都只提這件事，有別人在時，我也常常暗示他這件事。我老是說，他若敢在外面拈花惹草，那是多麼不要臉啊。」

P.115 從愛吃醋的雅卓安娜口中套出足夠的供詞之後，女院長說：「難怪妳的丈夫會發瘋。善妒的女人罵起來，比瘋狗咬人還兇。看來是妳鬧得他不能睡覺，難怪他會昏頭脹腦。他吃肉時要配妳的責罵吃，吃飯吵吵鬧鬧會消化不良，所以他才會發燒發熱。妳說他在做娛樂消遣時，妳也會鬧得他玩不下去，既然社交和休閒的樂趣都被剝奪了，他當然會悶悶不樂、絕望不安了。這樣說來，就是因為妳愛亂吃醋，所以才把你丈夫搞瘋的。」

露希安娜想替姐姐辯解，於是說姐姐指責丈夫時一向都很溫和，然後又對姐姐說：「別人這樣說妳，妳怎麼都不回話呢？」

P.116 但院長讓她看清楚了自己的過錯，她只得說：「經她這麼一說，我自己都想罵自己了。」

雅卓安娜對自己的行為感到慚愧，不過仍堅持要院長把丈夫交還給她。院長不許外人進修道院，也不想把那個不幸的人交給善妒的妻子去照顧，就決定要用溫和的方法來處理。她走進修道院內，吩咐人把大門關好，不讓他們進來。

在這多事的一天裡，因為這些孿生兄弟彼此酷似，所以造成了這麼多的誤會。另外，老葉吉所得到的一天寬限，也眼見要結束了。現在太陽即將西沈，日落時如果還繳不出罰款，那就只有死路一條。

葉吉接受執刑的地方就在修道院附近。院長剛走進院裡，葉吉就來到了這裡。公爵親自來監刑，他表示，如果有人肯替葉吉出這筆錢，他可以當場赦免葉吉。

P.117 這時雅卓安娜攔住這個悲悽的隊伍，高喊要公爵主持公道，嚷著院長不肯把她發瘋的丈夫交還給她照顧。就在她說這話時，她真正的丈夫和僕人大拙米歐從家裡逃了出來，他們也來到公爵面前請求伸張正義，申訴妻子誣賴他發瘋，把他監禁起來，又說明他如何把自己鬆綁，從守衛的監守下逃出來。

P.118 看到丈夫，雅卓安娜大吃一驚，她以為他人正待在修道院裡。

看到這個兒子，葉吉認定他就是那位離開他去找母親和哥哥的兒子，並且相信寶貝兒子一定會立刻為他付贖金。他用做父親的慈祥口氣跟他說話，心裡很高興，想著自己馬上就可以獲救。

然而讓葉吉驚愕不已的是，這個兒子說他根本不認識他。他當然會這樣說了，因為這個安提弗小時候在暴風雨中和父親失散後，就再也沒見過面了。可憐的老葉吉努力要兒子認出他來，他想，一定是自己太過焦急哀愁，變得怪模怪樣，所以兒子才會認不出他來，再不然就是兒子看到父親淪落至此，羞於承認。就在一陣混亂之中，女院長和另一對安提弗及拙米歐走了出來。看到兩個丈夫和兩個拙米歐就站在面前，雅卓安娜目瞪口呆。

**P.120** 這下子，這些莫名其妙、令眾人困惑不已的誤會，立刻水落石出了。看到這兩對安提弗和拙米歐雙雙長得一模一樣時，公爵立刻猜到這些離奇事件的原因了，因為他想到葉吉早上告訴過他的故事。他說，他們一定是葉吉的兩個兒子和孿生奴僕。

此時，還有一件意想不到的好事情，讓葉吉的一生獲得了圓滿。他早上被判死刑，還有那傷心訴說的往事，都在日落之前得到了快樂的結局——可敬的女院長表明身分，說她就是葉吉失散多年的妻子，是兩個安提弗慈愛的母親。

漁夫把大安提弗和大拙米歐從她身邊帶走後，她就進了修道院。由於她稟性聰敏，品德高尚，後來當上這家修道院的院長。當她好意收容一個不幸的陌生人時，也在無意中保護了自己的兒子。

**P.121** 這些失散已久的父母和孩子們興奮地互相祝賀，親熱地互相問候，一時之間，都忘了葉吉還被處了死刑。待大夥冷靜了些，大安提弗把贖金交給公爵，要贖回父親的性命。公爵很乾脆地赦免了葉吉，不肯把錢收下。

公爵陪同院長和她剛找回來的丈夫孩子，一道走進修道院，聆聽這快樂的一家人漫談他們苦盡甘來的圓滿結局。我們也不要遺漏了那對身分卑微的拙米歐的喜悅，他們相互祝賀問候，開心地恭維彼此的長相。在兄弟的身上看到自己長得這般俊俏（就像照鏡子一樣），他們好不歡喜。

**P.123** 經婆婆的一番諄諄教誨之後，雅卓安娜受益匪淺，從此不再疑神疑鬼或是對丈夫吃醋了。

小安提弗娶了嫂子的美麗妹妹露希安娜。善良的老葉吉和妻兒在以弗所住了許多年。雖然這些讓人困惑的事情是真相大白了，卻不能表示日後就不會再有誤會發生。彷彿是為了讓他們記住曾發生過的混亂，偶爾還是會發生一些可笑的混淆，這個安提弗和這個拙米歐，被誤認成那個安提弗和那個拙米歐，於是上演了一場輕鬆詼諧的連環錯。